THE
BOULEVARD
MONSTER

By Jeremy Hepler

For Tricia and Noah,
My two greatest allies

Prologue

For the Record

My name's Seth Fowler, and I'm not delusional. Not in my understanding of the role I played in the Boulevard murders, or in my understanding of what telling my story can accomplish.

Right now on Channel 10 Michelle Farmer is standing on my front lawn warning people that I should be considered armed and dangerous. There's a little picture of me in the upper right corner of the screen—the one from my DWI arrest ten years ago—and a phone number on the bottom for viewers to call if they know my whereabouts. A ten-thousand-dollar reward has been offered for information leading to my arrest. In the background, Detective Morrell and a large group of officers are moving in and out of my house, collecting evidence. They searched Ryan's apartment earlier this morning, my dad's house shortly before that.

Even if I were found and arrested and had my day in court, and even if I could afford the best lawyer Mercy has to offer, I would be found guilty. The evidence would be stacked too high. No matter how detailed my account, no matter how hard I tried to convey my true intentions, my testimony would sound too contrived, too incredible, for sensible ears. Jurors would never see me as an honest, sane, God-fearing man. I get that. I understand. I'm not writing this in hopes of clearing my name with the authorities or the public. I'm writing it so my wife Brianne and daughter Sera will know my side of the story. They need to know what happened to Ryan and my dad.

They need to know about Luther and the birds.

One

Corpse in a Burlap Sack

Luther's birds followed Randy to my duplex the night I discovered the corpse. I didn't know to look out for them at the time, or notice them when he arrived, but they were there. They had to be. Watching. Listening.

I did notice Randy's new cherry-red F-150, though. When he parked in front of the carport and gunned the engine, everyone on the block probably noticed. He stepped out of the cab and waited with the driver's door open. His hair was wet and neatly parted, his T-shirt tucked into his jeans.

I shook my head in disbelief as I approached him. He and I both worked for Howe's Construction Company, and although he made a little more money than I did, he didn't make enough to afford a new truck on top of his mortgage and child support payments. "How the hell can you swing payments on something like this?" I asked. "Don't they cost like fifty-thousand bucks?"

He smiled and stroked his mustache the cocky way he did when he was scoping out the female situation in a bar. "Unlike you, I know how to save money." He leaned in the truck cab and grabbed a six pack of Coors Light. "And I invest well."

I laughed. "Invest? You don't know shit about investing."

He handed me a beer. "Well, I invested six bucks in this beer, and I bet you'll agree that was a damn good investment."

I popped open my can and took a swig. "Pretty good."

"That's what I thought," he said, and we both chuckled. When my eyes slid to his truck cab, he stepped back and gestured at the open door. "Get in. Check it out. It's got heated seats, satellite radio, Bose speakers, built-in GPS, iPod connector. The whole shebang."

To say I was jealous would be an understatement. My '79 Chevy Silverado had 211,000 hard miles on it. The radiator was rusting out on the bottom, the transmission had started slipping, the air conditioner leaked Freon like a stuck pig, the windshield was cracked, the seats were patched with duct tape in multiple places, and the cassette player ate tapes if you tried to fast forward or rewind. My dad had given me the Chevy twenty years earlier, and I figured it would be another twenty before I could trade up.

I inspected the F-150 cab as Randy proudly looked on, and then we made our way to the lawn chairs under the carport where we sat and drank and talked about work and women like we had every Wednesday night for years. When Randy finished his third beer, he crushed the can and burped. "I need to drain the weasel before I hit the road," he said, and headed toward the front door.

My attention moved to his F-150. In particular, the chrome toolbox attached to the bed. As a man who relied on tools to provide for his family and stored his tools in tarp-covered paint buckets, I coveted any toolbox. After opening my last beer and taking a sip, I walked over to the truck to take a closer look.

I balanced my beer can on the bed's ledge, but as I reached to open the toolbox, I accidentally knocked it off, spilling beer all over Randy's hard hat and a burlap sack sticking out from under the toolbox.

"Damn it," I said, and righted the can. I grabbed a rag that was in the bed, wiped down the hard hat, and then wanting to make sure the beer hadn't soaked through the burlap sack, found the opening and looked inside.

It took a second to register what I saw, but when I realized it was a human ear covered by strands of light brown hair, I let go of the sack and jumped back.

I thought my mind was playing tricks on me. It was getting dark out. The sun had already dipped halfway below the horizon. The ear probably belonged to a stupid sex doll or Halloween mask or something. It wasn't real. It couldn't be. I shook the nerves out of my hands and opened the sack again. This time wide enough not only to see the ear and hair, but also a pair of brown eyes, girl's eyes. Eyes large enough to swallow the moon. And they seemed to be staring right at me, pleading for help. I felt a strong urge to run, to flee, to get as far away from the truck as possible, but I didn't. Instead, I closed my eyes, took in a deep breath, and told myself that I was just freaking out. There was no way she was a flesh-and-blood human.

To convince myself, I gently grazed my fingers through her hair, over her cheek. The hair felt soft and released a faint flowery scent, like it had recently been washed and conditioned. The skin felt smooth and cool, definitely real. Too real.

After glancing at the door to make sure Randy wasn't coming, I ran my hand over the rest of the sack, pushing down hard enough to feel bones beneath the little flesh clinging to her frame.

I pulled my hand away when the front door opened. Randy stepped out onto the porch but turned back around and yelled something to Brianne before looking my way. I quickly grabbed my empty beer can, hurried back to my lawn chair and plopped down.

It was no secret that Randy had a sketchy relationship past. He'd been divorced four times, and two of his ex-wives had told Brianne that he'd hit them. Likewise, one of his ex-girlfriends—a stripper who worked at The Yellow Rose—claimed he'd broken her nose and had a restraining order put on him. Maybe the girl in the sack was someone he'd met at a bar the night before. Maybe he'd gotten into an argument with her and lost his temper. He didn't weigh more than a hundred-and-fifty pounds with a bag of wrenches in his hand, but as tiny as she felt in that sack, it wouldn't have taken much to snap her neck or crack her skull. But if he did kill her, how was he acting so casual? So normal?

I felt like I sat there trying to rationalize the situation for hours, but it couldn't have been more than twenty seconds before Randy slapped my shoulder. "That woman of yours, she's a hoot, man."

Keeping my eyes locked on the bed of his truck, I slowly nodded.

He pulled his keys out of his pocket and grinned like his world was right as rivets. "Well, I've got places to be, and women to do. I'll see you in the morning."

I slightly lifted my beer can and managed a faint, "Okay," as he headed toward his truck. He'd made the *women-to-do* statement countless times over the years, but that night it took on a new meaning. A brown-eyed-dead-girl-in-a-sack meaning.

He fired up the engine, gassed it a few times, and honked the horn twice as he roared away with the windows down and the radio blaring.

I'd known Randy since our Mercy High days, and although we'd often butted heads at work and in leisure, we'd been through some sticky times together and I considered him a good friend. I wanted to give him the benefit of the doubt, I did, but my gut told me that the girl in the sack was real, and since the truck was fresh off the lot, no one else could've put her there but him. Still, I sat there for twenty or thirty minutes staring at the empty beer can in my hand before calling the Mercy Police Department.

A few minutes after I hung up, Brianne stepped out onto the front porch in her Snoopy pajama bottoms and a tank top. "Why are you sitting out here in the dark?" she asked, and turned on the porch light. "Dinner's ready."

I stood, and as I silently made my way toward her, she searched my face.

"Do you feel okay?" she asked.

I stopped a few feet in front of her.

"Seth, what's wrong?"

I looked back over my shoulder where Randy's truck had been parked, and when I met eyes with her again, I told her how I'd found the girl's body. What she'd looked like, felt like, smelled like. How real she'd seemed.

"Did you say anything to Randy?"

I shook my head. "I found her when he was inside using the bathroom."

"Did you call the cops?"

"I just got off the phone with them."

Whispering curses under her breath, she pulled a pack of Marlboro Lights and lighter out of her pajama pocket, lit up, and took a long, hard drag. "You know, it doesn't surprise me one fucking bit. If anyone we know is capable of killing someone, it's him." She took another long, hard drag. "What did the cops say?"

"They're sending someone over to talk to me," I said. "Will you go inside and keep Sera busy so she doesn't come out here?"

"Don't worry. She's in her room with the door closed. She claimed that she had so much homework she didn't even have time to come eat, so I took her spaghetti to her in there."

"Okay, but if she does come out here will you—" I broke off when an unmarked cruiser eased up to the curb in front of the duplex.

"If she comes out, I'll take care of it," Brianne said, smashing her cigarette out on the porch as Detective Morrell and Sergeant Adair made their way toward us.

Morrell was dressed in a black suit, had a trimmed mustache, and his silver hair was slicked down with enough grease to lubricate a front loader axle. I'd seen him on the news before, talking about a murder or drug bust or something.

Adair wore a tight Polo shirt and khakis, and appeared at least fifteen years younger than Morrell. His rigid posture, hardened eyes, and crew cut screamed military.

"Are you Seth Fowler?" Morrell asked.

"Yes."

"I'm Detective Morrell, and this is Sergeant Adair."

I shook both of their hands, introduced Brianne, and Morrell pulled a notepad and pen out of his coat pocket. "Okay, now will you start from the beginning and tell me everything that happened from when Randy arrived until he left?"

He took notes as I talked, and when I finished, he asked, "Exactly how many beers have you had tonight?" His voice had a casual Texas drawl, making the question come across matter-of-fact rather than accusatory.

"Three. Randy and I split a six pack."

"And you guys didn't do any illegal drugs?" Adair asked, his words coming out fast and clipped, definitely accusatory. "No pot or coke or anything like that?"

"No. Never."

Adair crossed his arms in front of his chest. "And you're sure it wasn't an old movie prop, or mannequin, or Halloween decoration? They make those things pretty life-like these days."

"I guess it could've been," I admitted. "But she looked so real. Her eyes..." I glanced down, remembering the way she seemed to be staring at me, pleading for help.

When I looked up, Morrell asked me how I knew Randy.

"We work together at Howe's Construction," I said. "I've known him nearly twenty-five years."

"Is he married?"

I shook my head.

"But he's been married four times," Brianne added. "And I know for a fact that he hit at least two of his exes. I can give you their names if you want. I'm sure they'd be glad to help."

Morrell jotted down the names as Brianne spelled them out, and then he closed his notepad and shoved it in his pocket. "We might have more questions for you later, but that should give us enough to go on until we find him and see what's in the back of his truck."

I nodded. "What do we do if he comes back?"

"You give us a call, without him knowing if possible, and we'll get someone here as quick as we can. I wouldn't worry about that, though. We'll put an APB out on his truck, and we should find him pretty quick. There aren't too many places to hide a new cherry-red F-150 in Mercy." Morrell extended his hand, and I shook it again. "We'll be in touch soon."

He and Adair headed back to their cruiser, and Brianne laced her fingers between mine and gave my hand a firm squeeze.

"This is fucked up," she whispered.

"I know. Let's not tell anyone about it until we hear back from the cops."

She agreed.

TWO

Bamboozled by the Bird Bandits

I reached the West Hill neighborhood ten minutes before eight the following morning. Ryan and the other guys were huddled around the makeshift shed we'd built the first day on the site, talking, waiting for their assignments. My boss Dan Howe was sitting in his Dodge Ram with the window down, watching them, slurping a Diet Coke. Randy wasn't there.

Dan lowered his cup and forced a smile as I approached his truck. He had taken the helm at Howe's Construction Company two years earlier after his dad had suffered a fatal heart attack, falling face-first into a slab of wet cement. Since then, Dan had lost half his hair, his body had ballooned to an enormous size, and he'd stopped smiling real smiles. When ribbed by some of the guys, he blamed his weight gain and hair loss on our lack of work ethic. When he left, we blamed it on his lack of cojones.

"Where the hell's Randy?"

I shrugged. "No idea."

Dan shook his head, took a loud slurp. "Are the footings set and everything square and level on 5305?"

"Yep. We're going to get the cap break and vapor barrier down this morning."

Another loud slurp, the last gurgling slurp. He poked the straw around in the ice. "You already got the rebar cut, don't you? Because Sparks should have the cement truck here around one."

I nodded. "Everything will be ready."

He glanced toward the shed, back at me. "We need these

houses completed before the end of summer, you know."

He'd told me that every day for six months, and I always told him we would. He wedged his cup between his thighs and put the truck in gear. "I've got to go make some calls about that wheelchair ramp project over at Splendor Elementary. I'll come back later or give you a call at lunch to see how everything's going."

As he pulled away, I made my way over to the shed where Ryan shot me a mischievous grin. Ryan was Brianne's younger brother, and I had helped him land a job at Howe's two years earlier. "Did he say if he was going to go jerk off or eat first?"

Although absent enthusiasm, I played along, like always. "He didn't. But my guess is that he'll jerk off first."

"I hope he waits until he gets back to the office," Ryan said. "If he tries to whip it out in his truck he might get stuck." He put his hair behind his ears, puffed out his cheeks, and widened his close-set eyes. Pretending he had an enormous gut, he struggled to reach his zipper. "I can do this," he said, mocking Dan's prissy voice. "I can do it."

Everyone broke into laughter, and a few guys gave him fist bumps. I flashed a brief smile, but kept my eyes on the dirt road leading to the lot where we parked our trucks. I wanted to know where Randy was, if he'd been arrested, and why Morrell hadn't called me yet. Once the laughter faded, I reminded everyone of their morning assignments and sent them on their way.

We completed the capillary break and vapor barrier around noon, and I was headed to my truck to grab my lunchbox when my phone vibrated. I fished it out of my pocket and checked the number. It was Dan. I answered, and as I told him about the morning's work, I noticed a scrap of paper on my driver's seat. I figured it was piece of trash that had blown into the cab because I'd left the windows down. But when I picked it up and turned it over, I saw a message addressed to Mr. Fowler. The words were written in fancy cursive letters that reminded me of my grandma's signature on the birthday cards she'd sent me every year until her death.

Mr. Fowler,

*I have a tremendous opportunity for you. Come
by Murphy's Coffee Shop tonight at 8 o'clock. If you
know what's good for you.*

I read the message and then jerked my eyes toward the shed,
expecting Ryan to be watching, waiting to see if I took the bait.
Pranks were a daily occurrence with him, and like everyone
else, I'd been on the butt-end of my fair share. But he wasn't
looking at me. No one was. He was standing in front of the shed
with his Soundgarden T-shirt pulled up over his head and his
hands flailing in front of him as though he were swatting at a
swarm of bees. Everyone else was sitting in the shade eating,
laughing at him.

I read the message again. West Hill was on the outskirts of
town, at least five or six city blocks from any other residential
neighborhood, strip mall, or gas station. There was no reason
for anyone other than us to be out there, and I'd checked the dirt
road leading to the site enough that morning to know no one
had come or gone. Which meant it had to be a prank. If I showed
up at Murphy's, I'd probably find a few skimpy-dressed girls
waiting for me—girls who'd been asked by Ryan to tell me they
needed a pimp or sugar daddy. That would be right up his alley.
Plus, he was the only person who ever called me Mr. Fowler.
Sometimes when I told him to stop jacking around and get to
work, he'd say, "Yes, sir, *Mr. Fowler.* No problem, *Mr. Fowler."*
Thick with sarcasm.

I set the note under the corner of my lunchbox on the hood
of my truck and pulled out my water bottle. I took a swig and
was eyeing Ryan for a telltale sign of his involvement when one
of the other guys yelled, "Look out, Seth."

Turning my head, I saw a blue jay dive-bombing my truck
like a falling lawn dart. Startled, I dropped the bottle, ducked,
and watched it pluck the note out from under my lunchbox
with amazing precision. Some of the guys who saw it happen

laughed as it flew away with the scrap of paper in its beak, others whistled. I stood and simply watched it go.

At the time I didn't think too much of it. Blue jays and pigeons had been a mainstay on the site all spring and summer. Many of them lived in a copse of cottonwoods by a pond about a hundred yards south of the site. During lunch break we'd always thrown scraps to them, and they'd quickly learned what time to arrive for an easy meal.

Often when someone had left their lunch unattended while they went to take a leak or make a private phone call, a courageous bird would hop over and snatch their food. Bamboozled by the bird bandits was what we called it. I figured the blue jay that dive-bombed my truck had confused the white piece of paper for a hunk of bread. I'd been bamboozled by the bird bandits. With flare. Nothing more, nothing less. It didn't occur to me until much later that he'd been watching me, waiting for me to finish reading the note, and that his presence was linked to Randy.

That evening I found a note from Brianne on the kitchen counter saying she'd gotten off work early and had taken Sera and one of Sera's friends to Johnson Park to swim. I was in the bedroom peeling off my work clothes when I heard a knock on the front door.

Checking the peephole, I saw Detective Morrell, flanked by Sergeant Adair. Morrell was sporting a brown suit, Adair, the same khakis as the day before but a different colored Polo shirt. The expression on both of their faces was blank. Wearing only boxers, I flung the door open and asked, "Did you find the body?"

Morrell pinched his lips and shook his head, keeping his droopy eyes glued to mine despite my lack of clothes. "No. We found tarps, buckets, and a bunch of other tools, but no burlap sack. No body."

"What did Randy say about it?"

"We can't find him."

"You can't find him?"

Morrell shook his head again. "We haven't found anyone who saw or talked to him after he left here last night."

"Well, he couldn't have just vanished," I said. "Where'd you find his truck?"

Morrell watched me for a moment, his bullshit detector on full alert. "We found it out at Jim's Lake. Abandoned near that cliff all the teenagers jump off of when the water's high enough."

"What do you mean abandoned?"

"The keys were in the ignition, the driver's door open," he said.

"And his cell phone was in the cab," Adair added.

My eyes bounced from Adair to Morrell, Adair to Morrell. "What do you think happened?"

Morrell shrugged. "Anything is possible at this point. He could've gone out there, or have been taken out there, for any number of reasons. Or, he may not have gone out there at all. His truck could've been dumped there by someone else. We're not sure. Did he mention anything to you about going out to Jim's Lake last night?"

"No. He didn't."

Morrell pulled out the same notepad from the day before and wrote something down. "Do you know if he went out there very often?"

"He fished and camped out there sometimes, like we all do, but that's about it."

"Did he ever take dates out there?"

"I think him and one of his ex-wives used to go out there to mess around, but that was fifteen years ago."

"Did he ever go out there alone?"

"Not that I know of."

Morrell scribbled a few more notes. "And you said when he left here he was in a good mood and had no idea you'd found... what you thought you'd found, right?"

"Yeah. He was acting the same way he always does. I figured he was going to Wizzards or some other bar when he left."

Morrell nodded and put the notepad away.

"I can't believe this," I whispered, shaking my head. "Where could he be?"

"We'll look until we find him," Morrell assured. "We have officers canvasing the lake area right now, and our forensics team is detailing the truck for fingerprints or any signs of a struggle. We hope to get a cadaver dog out there soon, too."

I eyed my bare feet for a moment, then met eyes with Morrell. "So you think he might be dead?"

Morrell shoved his hands in his pant pockets. "I've learned never to guess, son. It doesn't do any good."

"I don't think it's a good sign that he doesn't have his truck or cell phone, though. Do you?" Adair added.

The question momentarily rendered me speechless. My eyes fell to my feet again. I felt like I was dreaming, like I was in one of those NCIS shows Brianne religiously watched.

Morrell placed his hand on my shoulder, and I looked up. "Until we get evidence to the contrary, we're assuming he's alive," he said. "You just need to contact us if you see or hear from him, okay?"

"Okay."

Three

Luther's Subtle Touch

I didn't see Ryan's truck at Murphy's Coffee Shop or at the Wendy's next door when I pulled into the parking lot, but I assumed he'd make himself known soon enough. My plan was to let the prank play out, let Ryan and the other guys have their laughs, and then down enough beer at Wizzards to calm my nerves before going home and telling Brianne the latest news about Randy.

Inside Murphy's, three college kids were typing on laptops in the corner, two elderly women were chatting in front of the fish tank, and a middle-aged man was at the counter, ordering. I stepped in line behind him, bought a small coffee, and sat by the front windows where I could watch the parking lot.

While I sipped my coffee, another college kid with a laptop arrived and joined the others. The middle-aged man and the two elderly women left. A few younger women came and ordered ten drinks to go. The drive-thru stayed busy. But no one approached me or even looked my way. Just after sunset, I refilled my coffee, and figuring the prank had fallen through the cracks somehow, headed to my truck.

When I opened the door and the interior light popped on, I was shocked to see a thin man with olive-colored skin and an angular face sitting in the passenger seat. He had on black slacks and a white Guayabera. His eyes were blue as the midday sky, his slicked back hair black as oil.

Instinctively, I clenched my fists. "Who the hell are you?"

He extended his hand in a casual, generous manner, as if meeting people by breaking into their trucks was the norm. "Luther."

I held his gaze. "How'd you get in my truck?"

He eased his hand back. "You left it unlocked. You really shouldn't do that. It's not safe."

I didn't remember leaving it unlocked, but it wouldn't have been the first time if I had. "What do you want?" I asked.

"To give you the opportunity of a lifetime."

"*You* left the note?"

He gave me a confident, unbreakable smile. "Sit down." He patted the driver's seat. "Let's talk."

I scanned the parking lot and the windows at Murphy's, but didn't see any sign of Ryan or the other guys.

"Who are you looking for?" Luther asked.

I glanced at Murphy's again, back at Luther.

"Ryan didn't put me up to this," he said. "If that's what you're thinking."

"How do you know who he is then?"

"I know everyone I need to know."

I snickered, took my lucky Rangers cap off, ran my fingers through my hair. *Fucking Ryan.* "And what exactly is this opportunity?"

"Hop in, and I'll tell you all about it."

Ready to get the charade over with and head to Wizzards, I put my cap back on and sat down. After I shut the door, I noticed the cab smelled like fresh lavender. "You've got three minutes, Luther," I said, blatantly checking the time on my cell phone.

"Then I'll get right to it." He pulled a roll of cash out of his pocket and handed it to me. It was all hundreds, crisp and clean, and appeared to be real. But any fool with a good printer could do a decent counterfeiting job these days. "There's three thousand dollars there," he said. "If you accept my offer, you can take that home tonight as a good faith gesture."

Raising my brow in fake astonishment, I handed the roll back to him. He set it on the dash.

"What's this great offer?" I asked.

"In simplest terms, you get rid of some trash for me, and I pay you for it."

"Why can't you get rid of it yourself?"

He peered into my eyes for a long moment, as if I should know the answer. "I don't have the means anymore."

"What makes you think I do?"

"You construction guys have to get rid of trash all the time."

"Yeah. We pay to have it disposed of or recycled like everyone else."

His mouth crept up into a knowing smile. "True. But sometimes you just bury it on the site or dump it in undisclosed locations to save time and money, right?"

I checked the rearview mirror, still expecting to see Ryan somewhere close by, but he was nowhere to be seen. I sighed and continued to play along. "How much trash are we talking?"

"Not much. Maybe a hundred pounds at a time."

"You could just toss that in a dumpster."

"My trash can't be disposed of in dumpsters."

I chuckled. Here comes the punchline, I thought. "Why? Do you run a meth lab or something?"

He didn't answer, but the intensity in his eyes told me everything I needed to know. He was serious. This wasn't a prank. He wasn't Ryan's friend. Wasn't an actor. Ryan and the guys weren't waiting around the corner. He really did want my help. A lump materialized in my throat, and my mood instantly changed from annoyed humor to cautious confusion.

"You're not joking?"

"Do I look like I'm joking?"

I shook my head, forced the lump down. "I don't think I can help you," I said, fiddling with my keys.

"Oh, I think you can. I think you have to."

I met eyes with him. "I don't think so."

"You owe me."

"*Owe you?* I don't even know you."

"But you knew Randy." He paused, licked his lips. "And so did I. Well."

My eyes slid to the money on the dash, my thoughts to Randy. His new F-150. The big-eyed girl in the sack in the bed of his truck. His disappearance. My heart began pounding against my ribcage like a two-ton jackhammer.

"If you help me," Luther said, following my eyes and tapping the cash with his finger. "I'll pay you a thousand dollars a week for as long as we do business." I moved my eyes to him. "Do the math," he continued. "That's fifty-two thousand dollars a year. Think of what you could do with that. You could get your dad a nurse. Start a college fund for Sera. Help Ryan get out of debt. Buy Brianne the house she's always wanted. Replace this piece of shit truck that breaks down every other week. And," he paused, "you could finally get Esperanza a proper tombstone."

The tombstone remark hit a sensitive nerve. "How do you know about..."

My head was spinning, thoughts swirling with too many jumbled questions to finish just one.

"You deserve a better life, Seth. You're a good man. You've just never had the right opportunity fall into your lap. Well," He turned his palms up and spread his hands out in front of him as though the opportunity was a visible, tangible thing, and he was holding it. "Here it is. The opportunity to drastically improve your life. All you have to do is bury a little trash for me from time to time. Who in their right mind would refuse that?"

I stayed quiet, and Luther patted my arm. "I can give you and everyone you love a better life," he said. "Let me do that for you."

"I can't. I can't dispose of bodies like trash. You'll have to find someone else to help you."

"That's not an option I'd advise you take."

I inhaled a shaky breath and pushed it out, then glanced at the cash on the dash. "I think you're three minutes are almost up."

"Then I'll cut to the chase." Luther aggressively pointed at my chest. "You're one of the reasons we're both in this situation. If you don't want to end up like Randy, I suggest you rethink your decision."

"Is that a threat?"

"You're a smart man. I think you know the answer to that."

Before I had a chance to respond, he looped his slender fingers around my wrist. His grip wasn't tight and I was almost twice his size, but I knew that I couldn't pull away even if I tried. His power went beyond his flesh. Far beyond anything

I thought was humanly possible. He seemed to be touching not only my skin, but also my emotional core. I felt vulnerable. Exposed. Violated. Manipulated. Controlled. My chest tightened and fingers curled into fists as an intense feeling of guilt and fear coursed through my body.

"This doesn't have to be tough, Seth. You need to open your eyes. You're forty-four years old, and up until this moment in your life, you've been holding the short end of the stick. I'm giving you the chance to change that. Probably you're only chance. If you don't take this opportunity, you're not only shitting on your own future, you're shitting on your dad's, Sera's, Brianne's, Ryan's, their mom's, and anyone else's who could benefit from it. Do us both a favor and don't do that."

A thick curtain of silence fell between us that seemed to last forever. When I finally replied, my words came out weak. "How long do I have to decide?"

"Until I get out of this truck."

"I need longer than that. I need to think about it."

Luther shook his head definitively.

Staring into his eyes, which seemed to be faintly glowing, I felt helpless, cornered, terrified. I wanted him to let go of my wrist more than I'd ever wanted anything in my life. Eventually, I nodded once, accepting the offer.

Luther's mouth parted into that confident, unbreakable smile again. "So we have a deal?"

I nodded once more. He took his hand off my wrist, and a huge sense of relief came over me. As though an undeserved cross had been lifted off my back.

"Good," he said. "You made the wise choice. I think we'll work together well. We might even become friends." He opened the passenger door, stepped out of the truck, and looked back over his shoulder. His smile was gone. "If you ever tell anyone anything about me or our agreement, I'll know, and there will be severe consequences. For you and your entire family." He watched me for a long moment, said, "I'll be in touch soon," and then walked away.

For the next hour and a half, I sat in a dark corner in Wizzards chugging beer, replaying my conversation with Luther over and over in my head, fretting over how he knew what he knew, why he did what he did to that girl, and who—or what—he was.

I also thought about Randy, a lot. Based on how helpless and scared I'd felt when Luther had touched me, I couldn't imagine what Randy must've gone through when Luther killed him. It was a struggle to stop my imagination from running wild with the possibilities. I regretted being jealous of his new truck. I regretted wanting to take a closer look at that damned toolbox. I regretted opening the burlap sack. I regretted calling the cops. Because of me, he'd never buy a Harley and drive from New York to LA like he'd always dreamed. He'd never roof another house, catch another bass, drink another beer. Worse, he'd never hug his twin girls Jen and Julie again. Or take them for ice cream on their birthday. Or see them graduate high school, get married, or have kids of their own.

I've sent Jen and Julie birthday cards stuffed with cash every year since.

When I got home I hugged Sera long and hard.

Four

Dad-Daughter Movie Date Interrupted

Rumors about Randy's disappearance spread through Mercy like wind-driven prairie fire over the next month. Some people thought he'd been murdered by a jilted lover and buried in an unmarked grave. Some thought he'd staged his disappearance because he owed the government thousands in back taxes. Others thought he'd simply been drunk, drowned in the lake, and that his body would eventually be found.

I didn't tell anyone what I thought happened to Randy, and I didn't tell anyone about the ten one-hundred dollar bills I found in unmarked envelopes on my truck's dash each Friday morning, either. I hid the money with the other wad of cash Luther had given me in a duffle bag in my and Brianne's closet. I thought about it every time I was in my room, or anywhere else in the duplex for that matter, but I didn't spend a penny of it until I took Sera to see *Mockingjay*.

Like most soon-to-be eighth graders, she was obsessed with The Hunger Games. She'd read all three of the books and had a poster of Katniss and a sketch of Rue she'd drawn in art class pinned to the wall above her bed. For weeks she'd been reminding me that I'd promised to take her on a dad-daughter movie date to see *Mocking Jay* when it came out. I could count on one hand how many times he'd asked for anything special. To back out and blame it on a lack of money (the Chevy's transmission had been replaced a week earlier, sucking our bank account dry) wouldn't have been fair to her. Or honest. I had seven thousand dollars in a duffle bag in my closet.

I'd met Sera when she was six months old, her head already covered in bouncy black curls like her mom's. Esperanza Garcia, a petite, curvy woman with silky black hair, was having trouble reaching a box of cereal on the top shelf at Wal-Mart while holding Sera. I grabbed it for her, and we struck up a conversation. She'd moved to Mercy for a fresh start after her mom and boyfriend were killed in a bus crash in Mexico City. She lived in the same apartment complex as me, so I gave her my number and told her to call if she ever needed anything. Within a month, I was dating Esperanza, regularly babysitting Sera, and staying the night at their apartment three or four times a week. By the time Sera was eighteen months old, Esperanza and I had married at the Justice of the Peace, and I'd moved in with them. I officially adopted Sera three months later, nineteen days before Esperanza died. She was walking on the sidewalk at 4 AM, on her way to work at Sanchez Bakery, when a drunk driver swerved off the road and hit her.

The Saturday after I received Luther's fourth envelope of cash, Sera and I arrived at the UA Cinema shortly before the 12:45 showing of *Mockingjay*. She handed the clerk a twenty, told him we needed two tickets, and then turned to me, beaming. With her caramel-colored skin, unruly curls, and enticing eyes (which were growing too close to seductive for a protective dad's taste), she looked just like her mom.

Theater four was already packed, but we found two seats in the middle of the top section, halfway up. As the lights dimmed and the first preview began, Sera reached into her bag, pulled out one of the baggies of popcorn we'd brought from home, and set it in my lap. "There you go," she whispered.

"Will you hold onto it?" I passed it back to her. "I have to go to the bathroom."

"Okay, but hurry. You don't want to miss the beginning."

I nodded and hurried to the bathroom. I locked the door on the last stall and had just sat down when the bathroom door creaked open and someone else walked in. I stayed still as the footfalls moved closer and closer, louder and louder, and stopped in front of my door. Seconds later, the smell of fresh lavender seeped into the stall.

"You all right in there?"

My heart hitched.

Luther knocked. "Seth?"

I didn't answer. I was squeezing tight, biting down on my fist, trying not to go, but it didn't work. I went, quickly wiped, and flushed.

"Damn. What have you been eating?"

I stood, pulled up my pants, and eased back until my calves bumped the toilet.

"We need to talk, Seth. It won't take long. Meet me out at your truck when you're done."

I listened to him walk away and waited for the door to shut behind him before stepping out of the stall. My hands were sweaty, stomach tense. I splashed cold water on my face and stared at myself in the mirror. "You don't have a choice," I told myself. "You have to talk to him."

Luther was sitting in the passenger seat of my truck, wearing a grey Guayabera. He gave me a closed-lip smile when I sat down in the driver's seat. "I hope you're happy with our arrangement so far," he said.

I nervously glanced at him, the folded piece of paper in his hand, back at him, and nodded.

He smiled again, showing a sliver of teeth this time. "Good." He offered the paper to me. "This is for you."

I hesitated but took it, careful not to touch his hand. "What is it?"

"Some information you'll need in order to properly pay taxes on the money you're making."

I shot him a quizzical look.

"Your income's going to more than double this year, and you have to claim it all in order to stay off the IRS's radar. To help with documentation in case you ever get audited, you'll be paid with checks from now on. Twice a month instead of once a week."

I unfolded the paper and glanced at it. The word EnviroTek was printed across the top in block green letters. "What's EnviroTek?"

"It's the up-and-coming green technology company you invested in last year."

"Invested? I don't know shit about investing." The second those words hit my ears, an eerie sense of déjà-vu washed over me. I'd told Randy the same thing—*you don't know shit about investing*—the night I'd found the body in his truck.

"You don't have to," Luther said. "You just have to be able to make people believe your story."

"What's my story?"

He flashed his unbreakable smile. "About a year ago you decided Sera needed to have a college fund, so you started saving a little here and there. But when you looked into tuition costs and realized that you needed to do a lot more than just save, you paid an online financial consultant for advice, and he gave you a list of different investing options to look into. After some research, you found an up-and-coming green technology company that needed investors, and you decided to go for it."

I shook my head. "No one will buy that. Especially Brianne. She knows me too well. She'll know I'm lying."

"Then get better at it," he snapped back. "You have to make this work. You have to make her believe."

"You don't know Brianne. Even if I convince her, we barely make ends meet most months. She'll be so pissed that I've done all that behind her back she'll never forgive me."

"As soon as the checks start rolling in and most of your financial worries fade away, she'll forgive you. I promise. I've seen it a hundred times."

I looked down at the paper and read the name EnviroTek again. "And how do I explain the connection to Randy?"

"What connection?"

"The investment connection. He mentioned something about investing the last time I saw him. What if Detective Morrell and Sergeant Adair link my investment to his and—"

Luther waved his hand in front of his chest, cutting me off. "They won't. Other than the fact that you and Randy both invested a little money, which millions of Americans do every day, there's no financial link between you two whatsoever. Randy invested in storage unit chains. You invested in a green technology company. Just stick to the story I told you, and everything will be fine."

I ran my eyes over the cars lining the parking lot and stopped on a Scion with a blue jay standing on the driver's side mirror. At the time, I still had no idea the bird was watching us. "I don't know if I can do this."

"You have to. For your family." A beat. "You owe me."

The voice inside my head, the voice of survival and reason, agreed, assuring me I wouldn't live to see another sunrise if I didn't. I released a clutched breath and looked at him. "So what does EnviroTek specifically do? In case anyone asks."

Satisfaction danced across his eyes. "They manufacture solar panels, solar shingles, windmills of all shapes and sizes, greywater filtration and storage systems, and tons of other off-the-grid gadgets." He pointed at the piece of paper. "You can call the number on the bottom there and get an informative brochure if you want."

We sat in silence for a moment. My mind was racing, circling one thought in particular—how long until he'd want me to get rid of his trash. But I sure as hell wasn't going to ask him about it. I thumbed toward the theater entrance. "I better get back before Sera gets worried."

He nodded and extended his hand. "Business partners like us only have their word and handshake to solidify trust. I've upheld my end of the deal so far. Your handshake will show me you intend to do the same when the time comes."

Afraid a reminder of his power was coming my way, I cautiously eye-balled his hand.

"It's just a shake," he said. "You have my word."

I made eye contact with him, and when I shook his hand, felt only the smoothness of his warm palm.

Thank God.

Five

The Charade Begins

I waited until I received the first check from EnviroTek before I told Brianne about my investment. She was sitting at the round dining table that set half on the kitchen linoleum floor, half on the living room carpet. Still dressed in her Golden Coral shirt and black slacks, she was eating a peanut butter sandwich. Her dishwater-blonde hair was pulled up in a tight ponytail, exposing her high cheekbones and sharp eyes. She had little to no make-up on. Just the way I liked her.

I sat in the chair next to her and lay the check on the table between us.

"What's that?" she asked.

"A check."

She took a bite and spoke with a full mouth. "I know it's a check, but what is it?"

"Well." I clasped my hands together on top of the table. "I need to come clean about something." She stopped chewing and stared at me when I didn't immediately continue. I took in a deep breath, readying myself. I'd been rehearsing my story in the shower every night, and hoped she'd buy it.

"About a year ago I started saving money for Sera for college," I said. "But when I realized I'd never be able to save enough to make a dent in her tuition costs, I paid an online financial consultant for advice, and he helped me find some investment options. After some research, I found a company that makes solar panels and windmills that were looking for a few investors and decided to give it a shot." I waited for her to respond, but she didn't budge. "And now the company is doing great. Sales have more than doubled in the last six months."

She looked down at the check, specifically, at the amount. $2068.53 was more than she made in a month working forty hours a week, including tips. She chewed again, swallowed, then made eye contact with me, her eyes hinting at both anger and hurt. "Why didn't you tell me? You swore you'd never hide anything from me?"

We'd been dating ten years, living together for eight—long enough for me to know better than to give her an excuse, whether she asked for one or not. Any excuse for breaking a promise to her would've been a bad excuse and only given her ammo for an attack. I didn't want a war. I wanted a peace treaty, and to quickly move on. I told her I was sorry, had made a mistake, and begged her forgiveness.

"You should've told me," she said, dropping what was left of her sandwich on her plate. "I've never kept anything from you." She marched to the bathroom, slammed the door, and turned on the shower.

When she walked into the bedroom thirty minutes later, I was sitting on the edge of the bed staring at the check, hoping time and a hot shower had tempered her anger. She sat down beside me and hit me in the upper arm, hard. She had rail thin arms and legs but knew how to use her knuckles to leave a bruise.

"I guess." She glanced at the check. "I'll forgive you this once." Her eyes met mine. "But don't ever hide anything, and I mean anything, from me again."

"I won't," I said, rubbing my arm. "Especially if you're going to beat me if I do."

She laughed, and so did I. "Does anyone else know?" she asked.

"Of course not. I haven't told anyone but you."

She put her hand on my thigh. "At least I was the first." Her lips curving into a flirty, playful smile, she moved her hand up to my crotch. I parted her robe and slid my hand over her damp chest. "Where's Sera?" she asked, tilting her head as I kissed her neck.

"In her room. Listening to music and reading."

She pushed me off her, stood and let her robe fall to the floor. "Lock the door."

I obeyed, and then gently tackled her onto the bed. We didn't have romance-novel sex, but it wasn't a mindless animal fuck either. It was good, lustful, *we-are-two-thousand-dollars-richer* sex.

We were lying there afterward, looking at the check, talking about EnviroTek and what we could do with the money, when my cell phone vibrated. I scooped my pants up off the floor and pulled it out of my pocket. The caller ID showed a local number I recognized well.

Brenda Wilcox was a retired math teacher who lived next door to Dad. She'd also been one of my mom's best friends. When I was growing up, she'd been a staple in our house. Since she had never married and had no kids or siblings of her own, Mom invited her over for dinner nearly every night, and absolutely insisted she celebrate Christmas and Thanksgiving with us. The morning the cancer finally took Mom, Brenda was the one at Mom's bedside, holding her hand. Although she wasn't my real aunt, I'd always called her Aunt Bren.

"Hey, Aunt Bren. How's everything going?"

"Not so good."

She sounded tired. "Are you all right?"

"Oh, I'm fine. But when I went over to check on your dad after dinner and give him some cookies I baked, he was tearing through the house looking for a duck. He accused me of hiding it and was cursing at me so I left."

I put on my jeans and headed to my closet. "I'm sorry. He called my cell this afternoon, but I was busy at work and couldn't talk to him long. I should've gone by there after work."

"It's not your fault, Honey. He's just having a bad spell. It happens. I just wanted to let you know."

I threw on a T-shirt and my lucky Rangers hat. "I'll be there in a couple of minutes."

I hung up, and as I put on my socks, Brianne rolled out of bed and began to dress. "Is your dad all right?"

"He's flipping out about a duck or something. Cussing at Bren and blaming her."

"You want me to go with you?"

"No. You stay here with Sera. I'll give you a call when I get him under control."

Six

Lurth, Lummorville, and Duck

"Where'd you put it?" Dad yelled when I stepped into my childhood home. He was rifling through a pile of papers on the kitchen table. He was sweaty and wearing only red sweatpants. The little hair that ringed his head was frizzy and disheveled. Like a cartoon grandpa who'd stuck his finger in a socket. The living room was a disaster. Magazines and couch cushions and boxes cluttered the floor. The TV was blaring. I turned it off.

"Where'd I put what, Dad?"

"My duck."

I locked my hands behind my head and took a couple of deep breaths. In the nose, out the mouth. *Be patient with him* Dr. Hale had told me. "Where did you last see it?" I asked.

His hands stopped moving, and he looked at me. His lips were pinched with frustration. "If I knew that I'd know where it was." He went back to rifling through the papers. "Dumbass," he said.

I smiled at the name.

I was five years old the first time I remember him calling me a dumbass. He was in between jobs at the time and had been sipping cheap vodka all day. When I spilled chocolate milk on the carpet in front of the TV, he jerked me up by the arm, and screamed, "You clumsy dumbass. That's going to stain the carpet."

I started crying, and my mom rushed into the room. "Let go of him," she said. When he did, she pulled me toward her.

Dad pointed at the milk on the carpet. "Do you have the

money to pay for new carpet? I sure as hell don't."

"It'll come out," Mom insisted. "You're drunk. Get out of here."

Dad shot daggers at her with his eyes, and then stomped out of the house, revved up his truck, and sped off.

Mom led me to my bedroom and told me to lie down while she cleaned up the milk. When she returned a few minutes later, she sat on the edge of my bed and rubbed my leg. "You're not a clumsy dumbass," she said. "You're a Lummox, like me. Dad doesn't understand because he's not like us. We're from a different place than him, a special place, and we sometimes have trouble adjusting to our human bodies."

"What's a Lummox?" I asked.

"That's what we were called on Lurth."

Intrigued, I sat up and crossed my legs. "What's Lurth?"

"That's the planet we came from when you were a baby. We lived in a village called Lummorville."

"What did it look like there?"

Mom smiled. "Get your crayons and some paper, and I'll draw some pictures of it so you can see."

I hopped off the bed, grabbed my crayons, and ran to the dining table. For the next hour, we drew pictures of Lurth and Lummorville and talked about the differences between Earth and there. When it was time for bed, Mom told me the story of the day we left and came to Earth on a secret mission.

Over the next few years, I fully believed I was a Lummox, and my imagination ran wild with wonder and possibility. I made up stories about my Lummox relatives' adventures, covered my walls with pictures I drew of animals that lived on Lurth, and made my own Lurth clothing out of construction paper and cardboard that I wore when I played in the backyard.

I loved being a Lummox, thinking I was unique and special. But my Lummox life collapsed on the first day of first grade when I tripped and fell outside during recess and some kids laughed at me. Embarrassed, I told them I was a Lummox and *that* was why I'd tripped, which made them laugh even more, and one boy, Jake Collins, called me an idiot.

To prove I wasn't an idiot, that I was a Lummox, I pulled

a dictionary off the shelf in Ms. Scott's room after recess and flipped to lummox, expecting to find a definition I could throw in Jake's face. Instead, I found this:

lum-mox (lum-oks) n. (informal) a clumsy or stupid person.

I confronted Mom when I got home.

Disappointment flashed across her face. She squatted in front of me and said, "I didn't mean it that way. Sometimes definitions in a book are different than meaning. You know I don't think you're clumsy or stupid. I tell you that all the time." She put her hand on my shoulder. "And no matter how fake or stupid you think all the Lurth and Lummorville stuff is, it's still a very special, real place to me. Our place." She kissed my forehead. "You'll always be my Little Lummox."

That's why I smiled when he called me dumbass. It took me back to Mom and Lummoxes, and the very special, real place we called Lurth.

"What kind of duck was it?" I asked as Dad continued rifling through the papers on the table.

He grumbled and shook his head, as though my question were ridiculous. "My duck," he mumbled. "My duck."

Dad had been diagnosed with dementia two years earlier. At first I thought he was just becoming forgetful like most seventy-year-olds. He'd put his car keys in the freezer, forget to take clothes out of the dryer, not lock the front door, things like that. But when he got lost on his way to United, a grocery store he'd shopped at for fifty years, and had to call me for directions home, I knew something was wrong. Something more than regular aging.

He fought going to the doctor for a while, becoming angry and agitated if I brought it up. But one day after he was filling out some paperwork and couldn't remember his own birthday, he called me and agreed to see Dr. Hale.

Along with putting Dad on several medications, Dr. Hale advised him to hire a home assistant, or to move into a retirement community where he could have daily supervision, but he couldn't afford either. Other than his short stint in the army, he'd worked manual labor jobs his entire life, and his retirement plan was to work until he dropped dead. Shortly after diagnosis, he'd quit his job at Master Men Landscaping due to Dr. Hale's safety concerns, forcing Brianne and me to help pay for his utilities, taxes on the house, and supplemental insurance coverage.

I made my way down the lit hall to his bedroom. His bed was covered in junk he'd dumped out of plastic totes. As I refilled the totes, Dad opened a closet door in my old bedroom across the hall and started rummaging.

After stacking the totes in his closet, I sat on the edge of his bed and buried my face in my hands. They still carried the scent of Brianne's soap, her skin. "Duck, duck, duck," I whispered. "What does he mean? He's never been duck hunting. Maybe it was a postcard from an old army buddy or something. Did he ever..." Then it struck me like a bolt of lightning out of the clear blue sky. An image. A black and white photo of my dad and his mom and his beagle named Duck—the only dog he owned as a child.

I went across the hall and peeked into my old room. Mom had turned it into a sewing and craft room after I'd moved out. But now it looked more like an outdoor storage shed. There was a weed eater, a snow shovel, a trash bag full of crushed cans, and many unmarked cardboard boxes. "I'm going to the attic for a minute. I'll be right back."

"The ladder's broke." He replied without slowing in his closet search.

"All right. I'll see what I can do."

In the garage, I pulled down the attic door using the rope hanging from the handle, and a blob of July-hot air fell from the opening, carrying the smell of dust and wood. The ladder was supposed to unfold into a straight line, but the right side had snapped in two, making the lower half unable to support weight.

I found a flashlight on the shelf above the dryer, managed to bypass the lower rungs, and climbed into the attic. The last time I'd been up there was when I'd helped Dad and Brenda box up Mom's clothes and craft supplies a month after we buried her at Harrington Memorial Cemetery. I crawled on a slim plank passed the boxes with her name on them and shined the flashlight beam on what I was looking for. A white box labeled PHOTO ALBUMS.

Mom could fill a photo album quicker than most people could fill a glass with tap water. There were probably fifteen or twenty in the living room closet, and five or six more in the white box. They weren't all photos of the family. Some were of her garden from different years, or the sunset, or falling snow, or a blooming snowball tree she saw on her way to work. Holding the flashlight in my mouth, I balanced on the cross beams and hefted the box over to the plank. By the time I slithered back to the opening, dropped the box onto the garage floor, and jumped down, my shirt was soaked with sweat.

I carried the box inside the house and pulled out the grey photo album with a cowboy hat on front. On the second page behind a thin clear film was the picture. Dad, his mom (who died before I was born), and Duck were standing on a curb. Dad wore cut-off jean shorts and a white T-shirt and his hair was crudely cropped. His mom was wearing a lengthy dress, had shoulder length hair, and piercing eyes. Neither of them was smiling. Dad had his hand on Duck's head. They'd named the beagle Duck because his head was solid black, and the rest of his body was white save a dark patch on one side that resembled a tiny wing.

I found Dad in his bedroom dumping out the totes I'd just put away. I held the picture up for him to see. "Is this what you're looking for?"

When he saw it, the frustration in his eyes and tension on his face instantly disappeared. He snatched the photo out of my hand and headed to the living room. I re-packed the totes, put them away, and followed him. He was sitting in his recliner looking at the picture. His legs were kicked up on the footrest, eyes brimming with emotion. I didn't know what to say. Dad had never been good at discussing emotions, so I just let him have the moment.

I straightened up the house, turned off all the lights, heated up a meatloaf TV dinner, and headed back into the living room.

"I heated up a TV dinner for you. It's in the kitchen."

He briefly moved his eyes to me, nodded, then looked back at the picture. He looked lost in the past, swimming in a pool of distant memories. I turned on the TV and set the remote on the armrest of his recliner.

"I guess I'll get then," I said. He nodded again but didn't look at me. "I'll call you later."

Outside, the setting sun colored the clouds on the horizon gold and purple. Had Mom been alive the house would've been lined with three-foot sunflowers. The grass would've been dark green and thick. The hedge running along driveway would've been trimmed to a perfect rectangle. But the yard was more dirt than vegetation now. Nothing had been trimmed or mowed or watered for years. Considering the condition of the yard, I should've been more suspicious of why there was a blue jay in the dying oak tree. But I wasn't. I sat on the porch, puffed my cheeks, and pushed out a loud breath. It was a relief to be out of the house.

I was checking my cell phone to make sure I hadn't missed a call when Brenda called out my name. I met her halfway across the yard and hugged her.

"Is he all right?" she asked.

"Yeah. He was looking for a picture of a dog named Duck."

She smiled. She had a head of white hair, and her mouth and eyes were bracketed a couple of times over, but when she smiled, I could easily see the happy little girl she once was. "That's what it was then. I should've figured that out. I remember that picture of him and his mom and that dog. Your mom showed it to me once."

"Don't worry about it," I said.

She bit her lip, looked down. "I can't imagine what it must feel like to know that you're losing everything from your past. Everything that you are and were and will be." She glanced at the house. "I wouldn't wish it on anyone."

"Me either," I said, glancing at the house as well.

Following a short silence, she smiled again and asked how

Brianne and Sera were doing. I told her fine, and she said she wished we'd come visit more often and I swore we would. After exchanging appreciation for the beautiful sunset, I thanked her for helping with Dad, hugged her, and headed to my truck.

I didn't notice the small piece of paper crammed under the windshield wiper until I fired up the engine. I rolled down the window and grabbed it. My stomach turned to cement as I read the words written in fancy cursive letters.

Meet me at West Hill. Now.

Seven

Collaborative Burial

I'd never been to the West Hill site after sunset. I dimmed my headlights as I turned off 55th and slowly made my way down the dirt road. A Howe's cement truck, two backhoes, and a T300 Bobcat were the only vehicles in the lot where we parked on workdays. The only sign of life: a sole blue jay perched atop the Bobcat that flew toward the shed when I killed the engine and rolled down the windows.

Keeping my eyes on the dirt road, I anxiously waited. Five long minutes passed with nothing. Five more. I took the note off the dash and read it again. *Now.* Just before I looked up to check the road again, Luther slapped the hood of my truck, and my heart jumped up into my throat. I slammed my elbow into the horn and dropped the note.

Luther laughed loud as he approached the driver's side window. He had a burlap sack slung over his shoulder and carried it with ease. Like Santa Claus carrying a sack of toys. His Guayabera was even red and white. But I was certain his sack didn't have toys in it.

"Why the hell did you do that?" I asked.

"You should've seen your face, man." That unbreakable smile again. My back stiffened when he reached into the cab and picked the note up off my lap. "I see you got my note." He shoved it in his pant pocket. "You ready?"

"Ready for what?"

He narrowed his eyes to annoyed slits and opened my door. "Let's go get this over with. I've got a plane to catch."

He dropped the sack and took off toward one of the foundations we'd poured earlier that week. When he looked back over his shoulder and saw I hadn't moved, he ordered, "Come on."

I slid out of the truck, scooped up the sack, and held it against my chest. It was heavier than it had seemed when Luther had carried it. Seventy-five to eighty pounds I'd guess. As I hurried to catch up with him, I tried not to feel the shape of legs in my hands, a head against my chest. Tried not to think about the fact that I was carrying someone's kid. Maybe someone's wife or husband. But I did. I did. And I kept walking.

Luther stopped on the backside of the 5103 foundation where the ground was leveled off. I stopped beside him and set the sack on the ground. He was staring at the copse of trees in the distance where the bird bandits lived, smiling as if listening to something other than the crickets that were clipping the night's silence. Something mesmerizing. Something specifically for him.

I nervously checked the road to make sure no one was coming, then turned back to Luther. "Why did you want to meet me? I figured you wouldn't want to—"

He snapped his head my direction, and I broke off. "That I wouldn't want to be here when you did your job?"

I lowered my head but made sure to keep my eyes pointed away from the sack. "I figured—"

"You figured wrong. Maybe I wanted to be here because I like you, and I know it can be hard the first time."

To my ear he sounded sincere. Sympathetic even. I didn't know what to say. I kept my head down. Part of me believed him. The scared part that would've believed anything that meant I wasn't out there alone with whoever was in the sack. But my instinctual, survival self, the part of me that clearly remembered his threats and the power of his touch, believed he was there to make sure I didn't get cold feet or do anything stupid. Knowing what I know now, I think both parts of me touched on the truth.

"You're going to pour the cement for the back porch tomorrow, right?"

I looked at him. I wanted to ask him how he knew that. How he knew seemingly everything about me. Who I was. Who I loved. Where I was and would be. But I didn't have the courage for that yet. I cleared my throat. "Yeah," I said. "We are."

"Then that's where we'll bury the trash." He marched toward the makeshift shed where we ate lunch, and I lost sight of him. My hands and knees were shaky. I checked the road again, then looked back toward the shed. I almost glanced down at the sack, but thought better of it.

Luther materialized out of the darkness, and as he grew closer, I saw he had a shovel in each hand. He handed me one and started digging without saying a word. I watched him scoop and toss a couple of times before joining in.

We dug in silence, but I dug clumsily, constantly glancing at him and back at the dirt road, while he dug swiftly, seemingly relaxed and at peace. I'm pretty sure we dug the five-foot deep, three-foot wide hole fairly quick, but it seemed to take forever, each scoop of dirt seemingly weighing a hundred pounds. When we finally finished, I was out of breath and sweaty. Luther looked like he'd just woken up from a refreshing nap.

"Toss it in," he said.

Without looking directly at the sack, I picked it up, dropped it in the hole, and immediately started tossing dirt on it. I didn't want to give myself time to think about the body, or for Luther to say anything at all. I wanted to finish and leave and pretend it never happened.

We filled in the hole and smoothed and leveled it off in less than half the time it had taken to dig it. Afterward, Luther handed me his shovel. "Now that wasn't so hard was it?"

I took off my lucky Rangers cap, then looked at him and shook my head.

"Good," he said. "From now on, you're on your own."

My phone vibrated, and he glanced at my pocket. "It's probably your girl. She probably thinks you're out with some other hussy." He gave me a wide grin. I couldn't tell if he was grinning at the notion that women think that way in general, or that Brianne might think that about me.

Using the bottom of my T-shirt, I wiped my face and rubbed

my eyes for a moment. When I lowered my shirt, Luther wasn't there. I spun in a circle, searching, but didn't hear or see any sign of him. He was gone.

I put the shovels back in the shed and hurried to my truck. I didn't check my cell until I reached the lit Toot'n Totum parking lot on 55th. Like Luther had guessed, Brianne had called. She'd left a message saying she was worried about me. She'd talked to Brenda and knew I'd left my dad's house hours ago.

I didn't call her back. I drove to Wizzards and took two shots and chugged three beers before going home to tell her about Duck.

Eight

Blue Jays, Blue Jays, Everywhere

My first big purchase was Esperanza's tombstone. Sera and I drove out to Harrington Memorial Cemetery the morning it was placed. Harrington is located ten miles north of Mercy, and in contrast to the barren prairie that surrounds the rectangular lot, old elm and cottonwoods shelter the graves from the sun, and a quilt of green fescue covers the ground, coming to an abrupt stop at the fence lines as though it had been snipped with a giant pair of scissors.

I parked about twenty yards from Esperanza's final resting place and killed the engine. "You ready?" I asked.

Sera looked up from her new cell phone and smiled. Brianne had helped her add streaks to her bouncy hair the day before. The cream color matched her tank top. Paired with a black skirt and black shoes, she looked prepared to audition for the X-Men. She looked beautiful. "Yep."

"All righty. Let's go."

Sera snapped pictures with her phone as we approached the granite, half-circle tombstone, and I handed her the bouquet of stargazers we'd bought for Esperanza when we reached it. She knelt, laid the flowers down, and ran her hand over the tribal-themed design etched across the top of the tombstone—a design that matched a tattoo Esperanza had had on her upper thigh. "So awesome," she said. "What do you think?"

"I think your mom would love it."

"Me, too."

Sera traced her fingers over her mom's name.

"You want me to take your picture?" I asked.

"Sure," she said. She squatted, wrapped her arm around the back of the tombstone, and laid her head sideways on the arc as if it were one of her most treasured friend's shoulders. I snapped the picture, and then she took her cell phone back and examined it. "Looks good. My first picture with her since I was what…a year and half old?"

I nodded. Eleven long years ago. A different time. A different life.

Sera loved hearing stories about her mom. The only memories she had of Esperanza were still-shot images. And she wasn't sure if those were real memories or wishful ones based on the pictures we had. One of which—Esperanza dancing in the living room of our apartment—was in a frame on her dresser. My stories were her only link to Esperanza's past. When I'd tell her stories like the one where Esperanza gave our groceries to a homeless woman and her children sitting on the curb outside the supermarket, or the one where she'd slapped an old man after he'd smacked her butt as she passed by his pawn shop, Sera listened with wonder-glazed eyes.

I scanned the cemetery, stopping on my mom's grave in the distance. Before Mom had died twenty years earlier, she'd bought side-by-side plots and a double tombstone for her and Dad. I held up the dozen daisies we'd bought for her. Her favorite. "I'm going to take these over to my mom."

Sera was sitting Indian-style on the grass. "Is it okay if I stay here?"

"Of course. I'll be right back."

I propped the flowers on my mom's side of the wide tombstone, told her that I loved and missed her, and that I hoped she was having fun in Lurth.

The last time I spoke to her, the night before she died, we didn't talk about me, or her, or dad, or work, or anything else Earth-related. We talked about Lurth and Lummorville for the first time in years. For hours. We talked about the trees and animals and smells and colors. About all the weird relatives and adventures that awaited us when we returned. We even made up two new forms of transportation Lummoxes used— underground swimming tunnels driven by warm currents, and strap-on backpack wings. Before I left that night, after I hugged her, she asked me to do the Lurth handshake I'd made up as a child. I think she knew that was the last time I'd see her alive.

When I returned to Sera, she stood and handed me her cell phone. "Check this out." It was a picture of Esperanza's tombstone, and perched atop the arc, seemingly staring at the camera, perhaps even smiling at it, were two blue jays. "Cool, right?"

I nodded, at first not thinking much of it, but as I handed the phone back to her, I thought about the bird bandit blue jay that had stolen the note from under my lunchbox. Then the one on the Scion at the UA Cinema parking lot. The one in my dad's dead oak tree in his front yard. The one on the Bobcat at West Hill that night with Luther. These two on the tombstone. Right then an alarm bell went off inside my head. The blue jays were linked to Luther. I could've kicked myself for not seeing it sooner. They were his. They had to be. But what could they... were they—

"I think Mom sent them," Sera said, breaking my train of thought, her eyes alive with idealistic giddiness. "Blue was her favorite color."

"I think so, too," I lied.

Ryan and Brianne were sitting in the lawn chairs under the carport, smoking, when Sera and I returned home. Sera told them how beautiful the headstone was and how Esperanza had sent two blue jays to visit us. She showed them the picture, and then headed inside. I grabbed a bucket out of the bed of my truck, flipped it upside-down, and sat next to Brianne. She took one last drag and stamped out her cigarette butt.

"The tombstone looks great in the ground," she said. She'd helped me and Sera pick it out. "Those birds were cool, too."

I didn't respond. I was staring at the cracked concrete between my feet, zoned-out, picturing Sera's photo in my head. The two birds. Two smiling blue jays.

"Hey," Brianne said, nudging my arm. "You all right?"

I blinked away the image and looked at her. "Fine. Just a

little tired." I rubbed my eyes and thinly smiled. "It did look great. Sera really liked it."

She nodded, lit another Marlboro Light, and met eyes with Ryan. She gave him a prodding, *ask-him* look, and gestured my way with her head.

"What?" I asked.

Ryan flicked his butt out to the edge of the driveway, put his hair behind his ears, glanced at me, Brianne, back at me.

"*What?*"

"I told him about your investment in EnviroTek, and how well it's working out," Brianne admitted. "And we were talking and..." She raised her eyebrows at Ryan.

"I was wondering if you could help me invest some of my money, too?" he asked.

I knew the question would come sooner or later. Ryan had over fifteen thousand dollars in credit card debt due to impulsive choices he'd made in his late teens. A month after high school graduation he'd landed his first full-time job and quickly discovered how indiscriminately credit card companies lend money. Unfortunately, he glossed over the lend and interest parts. He bought a Jet Ski, which was wrecked within two months, a 60-inch flat screen, which was broken, an '87 Pontiac Firebird, which was absent a transmission and sitting on cinderblocks in his friend's backyard, and gobs of clothes that were out of style and forgotten. I wanted to help him. But I couldn't in the way he wanted.

"I don't think I can."

Brianne's face scrunched in disbelief. She propped her left hand on her hip and eyed me like I'd refused to give Ryan a needed kidney. "Why not?"

We all looked upward when something clanked on top of the carport. Several small scraping sounds followed. A second later, a blue jay flew to the ground in front of the small crab apple tree in the neighbor's yard. I watched it, and it watched us.

"Well," Brianne said, her voice raising an octave. "Why not?"

"Please," Ryan said. "You know how much debt I'm in. It would really help."

"Yeah," Brianne added, taking a drag. "He could finally move out of Mom's place and get an apartment of his own."

I curled my lips in on one another and shook my head. "I'm sorry. My hands are tied. I don't think the guy who runs EnviroTek wants to add investors until the company grows more."

"Will you at least email him and ask?" Brianne said. "You're the one that helped his company grow by investing in the first place, right?"

"I guess I can," I lied. "But I don't think it'll matter."

"I'd appreciate it," Ryan said.

"If it doesn't work out, could you try to find something else for him to invest in?" Brianne asked. "Maybe another company like EnviroTek?"

I watched the blue jay flitter up into the crab-apple tree and work his way into a shady spot, facing us. Then I looked at Ryan. "Listen, you know I'll always help you anyway I can, but I don't know shit about investing. I got lucky. Plain and simple. I don't have any investment tips for you, and I never will." I glanced at the bird, back at Ryan. "I'm sorry. But I can go to the bank on Monday morning and get you a thousand dollars to put toward your bills, if you want."

"I don't know." Ryan shifted in his seat, straightened his cut-off khakis. I'd given him money before—twenty dollars here, forty dollars there—but never that much. When he made eye contact with me, he looked as serious and mature as I'd ever seen him. "I'll definitely pay you back."

I smiled. "No need, compadre."

Relieved, he smiled back. The statement was common with all the guys at work. I'm not sure who started it (or why we all said it with a cheap Spanish accent), but anytime one of us had forgotten our lunch or didn't have cash for a beer or two at Wizzard's after work, it became customary for whoever helped them out to answer any promise of pay back by saying, "No need, compadre."

As my attention shifted to the bird again, my phone vibrated. I pulled it out of my pocket and checked the number.

"Let me guess," Ryan said. "Dinosaur Dan?"

"You know it." I stood and puffed out my cheeks, slightly squatted, and pretended to reach around my giant belly to adjust my pants. Like Ryan always did. "Seth," I said in a weak prissy voice. "We need those houses done now."

Ryan jumped up and bested my lame impersonation. "I won't be able to properly eat and jerk-off until they're done."

Brianne smacked Ryan's arm and broke into hysterical, eye-watering laughter.

I laughed, too.

Following two plates of Brianne's spaghetti and plenty of beer, I walked Ryan outside. We stopped at the edge of the yard next to his small, mustard-colored Toyota truck. It wasn't night-black yet, but a few stars were visible. The moon was nowhere to be seen.

Ryan lit a cigarette. "I can't wait for fall. It still feels like a hundred fucking degrees out here."

"Probably is," I said, scanning the crab tree for birds.

He took a puff and punched my arm. He's the one who'd taught Brianne how to use her knuckles. I popped him right back. "Owe," he said, and chuckled. "I'm going over to Wizzards for a few more beers. You want to come?"

"Can't," I said. "Brianne rented a movie, and I promised to watch it with her."

"Is it a chick flick?"

I shrugged. "Probably."

He rolled his eyes, took a long drag, and blew the smoke upward. "I hope I'm not as whipped as you when I'm your age."

"Don't worry." I popped him in the arm again. "I don't think you'll ever be whipped. When you're my age, I'm sure your dumbass will still be chasing ditsy twenty-year-olds with big tits."

He chuckled again. "Probably so." He gestured at my truck, which was parked curbside behind his. "Looks like some Jehovah's Witness or Church of Christ freak left you a flier. They want to save you from the fires of Hell." With his cigarette dangling from his lips, he threw his hands theatrically into the air and wiggled his fingers. "Eternal damnation. Woohooo."

I looked at my windshield and saw the paper under the wiper. Before I could respond, Ryan headed toward the Chevy. He was reaching across the hood for the paper when a blue jay swooped down out of the sky, dive-bombing at his head. He squealed, dropped his cigarette, and fell back onto his backside. He closed his eyes and feverishly swatted at the bird as it circled his head like a shark circling prey in shallow water, plucking at his long hair.

I watched in amazed, terrified awe. The bird was protecting the piece of paper. It was protecting Luther. It was protecting me. I quickly ran around to the driver's side of my truck, snatched the paper off my windshield, and shoved it in my pocket. Then, right on cue, the blue jay flew toward me wearing a horrific grin, soared over my head close enough for its feet to rub the top of my hat, and disappeared into the night sky.

Ryan jumped up. "Holy shit! Why the hell didn't you help me?"

"What was I supposed to do?"

Ryan put his hair behind his ears, looked down, shook his head, and then laughed so hard he snorted and doubled over. When he rose up, he said, "That was fucked up, man. What's up with blue jays lately? Why'd it do that?"

To keep you away from the note, I thought. But I said, "Probably wanted some of your hair for his girl's nest."

"Shit. I'm going to get a fucking hair cut tomorrow if the birds around here are that high up for good nesting materials."

I tried to fabricate a genuine smile. Ryan pulled a pack of Marlboros out his pocket and lit up, the cherry momentarily lighting an orange circle in the center of his face. "I feel sober as a stick now." After a few puffs, he gestured toward my truck with his cigarette. "What happened to the flier?"

"You were right. It was a stupid Church of Christ thing." I shoved my hand in my pocket and wrapped it around the piece of paper. I needed to change the subject, quick. "You supposed to meet one of your regular girls at Wizzards, or are you looking for someone new tonight?" Ryan loved talking about women.

He'd talk your brain numb about all the ones he'd fucked if you'd let him.

"I'm always looking for new ones," he said with an air of cockiness.

"You better get going before all the hot ones are spoken for."

He took a drag and shot me a confident smile—a smile reminiscent of Luther's. "I'll get any hot one I want. You know that."

I shook my head and sigh-said, "Whatever."

He got into his truck and rolled down the window.

"Be careful tonight," I said.

"Will do, *Mr. Fowler.*" He winked, took a drag, and flicked his butt onto the road. I stepped on it. "Have fun watching Julia Roberts cry, or get cancer, or realize after two hours she really wants to fuck her best friend." He turned the key in the ignition and the engine sputter-started. He was in need of a new truck as much as I was.

He drove away, and I took the note out of my pocket. My sweaty hand had smeared the ink but the message was still legible.

Get rid of the trash.

I walked toward the tailgate as slow as a death row prisoner on his way to the execution room. The street light overhead highlighted the corner of a burlap sack that was wedged between a chunk of sheetrock and a cardboard box full of nails. I turned my back to the truck and read the note again, wondering how he'd gotten the sack there. When, exactly.

I looked up when I heard a bird circling overhead. It was a blue jay—the same one that had attacked Ryan, I assume. I'm not sure what compelled me, but I raised the note high over my head. A few seconds later, the bird plucked it out of my hand and flew away, bringing gooseflesh to my arms.

I rolled down the windows on the way to West Hill to rid the cab of the stress-sweat stink. Alone with the emotional pull of the corpse, my paranoid, guilt-stricken thoughts were magnified. Every pair of headlights that turned onto the road behind me seemed to have a siren box on top. Every driver in the oncoming lane seemed to slow and eye me, wanting to know who I was, where I was going.

Why I had a dead body in the back of my truck.

I parked next to a Howe's cement truck and exited the Chevy. West Hill was in the final stages of development. All but two houses were complete, and we were going to lay sod on the odd numbered yards the following morning; one of which, I'd decided, would be the burial site. Before I grabbed the sack, I looked across the neighborhood that would soon be filled with SUVs, swing sets, trampolines, dogs, joggers, the laughter of kids.

I thought about leaving, taking the sack to the cops and telling them everything about Luther. I thought about going home and spilling my guts to Brianne. I thought about getting in my truck and driving, and driving, and driving, until I could think of something better to do. But then I thought about Luther's touch. His power. His threats. The blue jays. Randy. I was in way over my head. I thought about Sera and Dad and Brianne and Ryan. All the good the extra money was doing for them. How much I loved seeing them happy.

Teetering under the burden of worry, I looked down at the sack, and advice Mom had given me when I was kid, when I'd complained about mowing the lawn, or doing homework, or cleaning my room, unexpectedly found my inner ear.

"Just get it done," she'd said. "And then you don't have to worry about it anymore."

I took a deep breath, lifted the sack out of the bed, and headed for the chosen lawn, trying to focus solely on how to complete the task as efficiently and quickly as possible.

Just. Get. It. Done.

I knew the Bobcat would make some noise, but I also knew no one was close enough to hear. On my way to the Bobcat, I noticed three blue jays standing on the roof of one of the houses. They hopped along the gutter as I passed. Watching. Listening. One of them flew down and landed on top of the Bobcat when I punctured the soil.

Twenty minutes later I had the sack buried, the dirt leveled, and the Bobcat back where it belonged. The bird who'd been on top of the Bobcat while I worked had rejoined the other two on the roof. I nodded at them to let them know I understood their purpose, hurried to my truck, and left.

Of course Mom's words didn't ring true that night. After the job was done, I still worried. I worried until I passed out drunk on the couch in front of the muted TV an hour before sunrise.

Nine

Mandatory Team Building

The next note came two weeks later while I was inside Cecilia Collier's apartment.

Cecilia was Brianne and Ryan's mom. Two days earlier Brianne had told Cecilia about EnviroTek, and Cecilia had immediately asked us for cash to buy a new bed, claiming the air mattress she'd been sleeping on for years irritated her back. But Brianne and I knew better. We'd given her money to buy a new bed the previous Christmas, and she hadn't bought one. She'd blown the money on liquor, cigarettes, and fast food, as usual. So this time, Brianne and I went to Marv's Furniture Store and bought a queen-size bed and Tempur-Pedic mattress ourselves. I met the delivery guys at Cecilia's apartment the next day on my lunch break because both Cecilia and Brianne had to work and couldn't be there. After the delivery guys left, I was crossing the parking lot, headed for my truck, when a blue jay swooped down and landed on the Chevy's hood. A note was wedged in its beak. My chest tightened as I plucked the note from the bird's beak. I dreaded what it would say, what I would have to do. I wasn't ready for another burial.

I read the message and sighed in relief. Luther wanted to meet at Abuelo's Burrito Extravaganza after sunset. I wasn't excited to see him again, but at least there wasn't a corpse in the bed of my truck.

I passed the note back to the bird and watched it fly away.

I didn't bother going inside Abuelo's. I parked in the side lot, out of view from 45th street traffic, and rolled down my window, allowing the smell of the coming rainstorm to invade the cab. For ten minutes I watched lightning flicker in the western sky, highlighting the rolling wall-cloud, listened to distant thunder rumble, and thought about Mom.

When I was a kid, Mom and I would sit on the back porch swing, listen to a weather radio, and watch the thunderstorms roll in. She taught me how to count the seconds between seeing lightning and hearing thunder to estimate how many miles away the storm was. They came and went so fast, the winds often shifting direction or intensifying to more than fifty miles per hour in a single gust.

As I sat in my truck that night, remembering, one of those strong gusts burst through the cab, nearly knocking off my lucky Rangers hat. I quickly rolled the windows up all but an inch, and as I was readjusting my hat, Luther opened the passenger door.

"Why haven't you bought a new truck yet?" he asked as he hopped in, carrying the scent of lavender with him.

Brianne had asked me the same question many times. But every time I passed a car lot and allowed myself to look at the new line of trucks, I thought about Randy and his brand-new cherry red F-150. A truck that was parked in the police impound lot in north Mercy. The guilt that would come along with buying a new truck wasn't worth it. I would never enjoy it. But I couldn't tell Luther that. I shrugged, watching the first raindrops splat the windshield. They were fat as dimes. "Just haven't gotten around to it."

"Well, you should." After a short pause, he asked, "Did everything go okay out there last time?"

I had no desire to revisit the experience. Besides, his birds had kept their beady little eyes on me the entire time. "Don't you already know the answer to that?"

He chuckled. "I meant emotionally."

I had no desire to revisit that night's emotions, either. Ever. I rolled up my window the last inch, flicked on the windshield wipers, then met eyes with him.

"It will get easier the more you do it," he said. "I promise."

I stared at him for a moment, fearful of what it would mean about me if the job did get easier. If I began seeing and treating the bodies like he did. Like trash. "Why did you want to meet?"

He rubbed his hands together as though he needed to warm them. "I wanted to talk to you about having a team-building."

"Team-building?"

He pulled his knee up on the seat, laid his arm across the top of the backrest. His hand was inches from my neck. "You know, when a team hangs out and bonds somewhere away from the job. Like you Howe's guys do when you have drinks at Wizzards after work."

Thunder boomed and shook the loose back window, and the rain intensified.

"But for me and you," he said, angling his head down and eyes up, "I have something better in mind."

An uneasy feeling stirred in my stomach. "What?"

He took a slip of paper out of his back pocket and handed it to me. "I have a cabin in Colorado. I want to take you there for the weekend." He tapped the paper. "That's all the information you'll need to buy a plane ticket, get a rental car, and get to the cabin."

I gulped down the uneasiness that was pushing its way up my throat. "I can't just leave for the weekend. What would I tell Brianne?"

"For such a smart man, you sure have problems coming up with excuses for your lady."

"I told you, I don't like lying to her."

"Then don't. Tell her you're going to meet with the other EnviroTek investors, which isn't a lie, and that we're going to discuss advancements in the business and 401K options, which we can do so that won't be a lie, either. You'll only be gone one night."

I looked down at the piece of paper and listened to the rain slow down as quickly as it had sped up as I gathered the courage to ask: "How do I know that?"

"Know what?"

"That I'll only be gone one night."

When I looked up, he leveled his eyes at me. "You think I

would help you the way I have just to take you out there and kill you?"

"I don't know."

"Nothing will happen to you as long as you keep your end of the bargain. Simple as that."

"Randy kept his end, and..."

Luther's eyes lit with fury, the blue seeming to glow a bit. "I was lenient with Randy. He was lazy. Sure, he didn't tell you about the trash, but he wasn't even supposed to have it with him. It was supposed to have been buried the night before. By being careless enough to allow you to find it, he broke the deal. In my book, it was the same as telling you."

Quick as a snake strike, he grabbed the back of my neck. His fingers were fire hot. A surge of shame and guilt seized me. I couldn't think or move. Only feel. Emotionally. Feel what he wanted me to feel. Like a school boy who was wrong to falsely accuse authority. A school boy fearful of what punishment he'd earned for daring to question his master's actions.

He removed his hand, took his leg off the seat, and turned his attention east, toward the backend of the storm. The clouds lit bruise-purple with each lightning strike. "You will return home happy and healthy as long as you don't do anything stupid. Are we good?"

Emotionally rattled, I couldn't find my voice to answer. He took my silence as a confirmation, which it was.

He opened the passenger door. A cool breeze carried in a thick rain scent. The temperature outside had dropped ten degrees or more. He stepped out of the truck and looked back over his shoulder, that unbreakable smile decorating his face. "Don't worry. We'll have fun," he said, and walked away.

Ten

The Naked Colorado Man

I'd never flown on a plane before, or visited Colorado. Hell, I'd only crossed the Texas border three times: the three trips I took with Mom to Oklahoma in our brown Station Wagon to clean out Grandma's house and settle her affairs after she died.

Brianne had never been on a plane or to Colorado, either. Many times while lying in bed at night we'd talked about using some of our money to go on a vacation. A real vacation. Not camping at Jim's Lake or hiking in Palo Duro Canyon. Her dream destinations were the classics out east—the White House, Empire State Building, Statue of Liberty, places like that—but when I told her about the Colorado EnviroTek trip, her mouth parted in surprised joy, and she said Colorado sounded great, too. "Me and Sera can go with you," she'd said. "We'll shop and go sight-seeing while you're in meetings, and then we can all spend the evenings together. Eat at fancy restaurants. Buy cheesy souvenirs. It'll be fun." It was hard. I didn't want to go alone, and I didn't like upsetting her, but I told her that I had to go alone. "My plane ticket is already purchased, and the rented cabin isn't big enough for our families," I'd lied. I promised to take her and Sera to D.C. for Thanksgiving to make up for it. She liked that.

The plane landed at Denver International Airport mid-morning on a Saturday. Avis's rental booth was right next to the baggage claim. I'd arranged to rent a four-wheel drive Tahoe because the weathermen had predicted a snowstorm Sunday morning.

The driving directions on the slip of paper Luther had given me led me southwest of Denver on Highway 285, deep into the Rockies. I wound through the mountains for about an hour before I reached the Pike National Forest sign and souvenir shop where I was supposed to stop. When the ten-foot-tall sandstone sign came into view, I saw Luther standing in the shade of a conifer tree in the souvenir shop parking lot to the right of it. His arms were crossed, and he was wearing a bright blue coat, black ski pants, and a wide-brim hat. Clouds of white breath blurred his face with each exhale. I pulled up next to him and he got in.

"Glad you made it," he said. "How was the flight?"

"Fine."

He nodded and smiled.

"Where are we going now?" I asked.

"Just keep heading south. I'll show you where to turn." As I pulled out onto the highway, he tilted toward the middle console, out of the sunshine cutting through the passenger window, and turned on the radio. He stopped on Steve Miller Band's *Joker*. "I love satellite radio. I couldn't pick up any stations out here before. You like classic rock?"

"Some of it," I said, shifting closer to the driver's door, away from him.

Eleven classic-rock songs later he had me turn south onto a thin paved road with a steep incline, then right onto a dirt road that wound up the mountainside. We eventually passed a faded PRIVATE PROPERTY NO TRESPASSING sign and made a left. As we navigated the maze of dirt roads, taking a left here, a right there, he sat perfectly still, whistling to tunes by The Doors, Lynyrd Skynyrd, and others. He seemed free as a bird, just like the Skynyrd song. I felt the opposite. Like a prisoner.

Shortly after we took another right, he pointed at a rectangle-shaped, two-story cabin and said, "There it is. Park on the side, under that carport."

The cabin faced west, the second-floor balcony looking out over a forested valley that was large and deep enough to conceal a herd of elephants. Staring at the sun shining down on the endless mountains in the distance as we headed toward the front door, I stumbled over a stone and dropped my duffle bag. He chuckled. "Be careful. This place can be hypnotizing."

He led me inside and to a bedroom next to the staircase, told me I'd be sleeping there, that he was going to change clothes, and that I could look around if I wanted. I tossed my coat and duffle bag on the queen-size bed, quietly checked the dresser drawers and closet and found them empty, did the same with the medicine cabinet and drawers in the en suite, then peed and headed upstairs.

The upper level was one single area—an open concept kitchen/living room. The kitchen had two ovens, a large oval island, and a walk-in pantry. The granite counter tops and stainless-steel sinks looked brand new. Two white leather couches, a matching recliner, and a flat screen on the wall decorated the living area. A wall of floor-to-ceiling double-paned windows looked out onto the balcony, the valley, and the mountains beyond.

After glancing down the staircase to make sure he wasn't coming, I quickly nosed around a bit, opening cabinets and drawers in the kitchen, checking the pantry which was filled with enough food for a family of ten, and then walked to the balcony windows and gazed at the endless wall of mountains in the distance.

"What were you looking for?" Luther asked when he appeared at the top of the stairs. "I heard you opening and closing drawers."

I looked back over my shoulder at him. He was buttoning the top button of his Guayabera. "Just looking around," I said. "Checking out the quality of the materials. You know, construction worker habit."

"I see." He opened the pantry door. "You hungry? We got tons of food."

I turned my attention back outside and noticed a blue jay standing on the balcony ledge. "No," I said.

"Thirsty? I got whiskey, beer, water?"

"Beer's good."

I watched a second bird land on the ledge, and watched them watch me until Luther tapped my shoulder and handed me a bottle of Dos Equis. "Thanks," I said.

He nodded and took a pull from his bottle. I chugged half of mine, sat down on the couch, and chugged the rest. He brought me another, then sat in the recliner. "Want to watch some TV? The satellite usually works well out here."

I shook my head.

"Play darts? I got a board in the garage." He thumbed toward the staircase.

I shook my head again and took a swig, watching the birds out on the balcony. There were four now. He followed my gaze. "You want to ask me something about the birds?"

The curious, imaginative, Lurth-loving kid in me had a hundred questions to ask. Like how exactly he was connected to them, how he controlled them, if he could read their thoughts, if they understand his words, if he could see through their eyes and hear through their ears like that guy on *Beast Master*. But the fearful adult in me wanted to know as little as possible, wanted to forget they existed at all. "I think I know enough about the birds." Another swig.

A sly smiled creased his face. "Oh, you do, huh? What do you think you know?"

I finished my second beer. My legs were jittery, eager to move. I went to the fridge and grabbed another. "I know they work for you," I said as I popped the top and made my way to the large windows. "That's all I really need to know."

Luther stood and stepped to my side. "I prefer the term *with* me, not *for* me." He touched my shoulder, and I snapped my head sideways. "They won't hurt you," he whispered softly, as though revealing a sensitive secret. I tried to step away from him but he squeezed my shoulder tight. "You need to relax," he whispered. "I won't hurt you, either." His breath was cool on my sweaty neck.

Beneath his hand my skin warmed and a feeling of comfort washed over me. A soothing, secure, protected feeling I hadn't experienced since I was a kid and my mom would snuggle with me in bed after I'd had a nightmare or when I was sick. My paranoid thoughts settled. My tense muscles relaxed. Consumed by peace and relief, I took a slow breath up my nose and let it fall out my mouth. I felt like I'd just arrived home from a long treacherous journey and laid eyes on Brianne's and Sera's smiles for the first time in years.

"We could be friends if you'd allow it," Luther whispered.

I raised my bottle and took a small sip. "Have you always been able to do this to people?"

He removed his hand, opened the balcony door, and walked to the ledge where the blue jays waited as though I hadn't spoken. One of them hopped into his open hand and nuzzled its head against his raised finger. He stroked the bird's back with all the gentleness of a mother caressing a newborn and whispered something I didn't understand.

With the calm feeling he'd forced into me fading, I finished my beer and headed to the fridge for another. When I came back, he was still petting the bird. I stepped out onto the balcony behind him and ducked my head so my lucky Rangers cap would block the cold wind nipping at my face. He set the bird on the balcony ledge and turned to me. "Let's go inside," he said. "I'm getting cold."

He went into the kitchen, and I sat on the couch and drank my beer. A few minutes later, he brought me a glass filled with Southern Comfort and ice to replace my beer. He sat in the recliner, and we drank and looked out the windows for a long while, watching the sun set and the stars reveal themselves. Eventually, he swirled the ice cubes in his empty glass and raised it head-high. "You want another?"

"I'll get it." I stood and took his glass. "I need to pee anyway." When I returned, all the window blinds were closed. Luther was lightly rocking in the recliner. I handed him a glass of whiskey and sat down on the couch.

"You don't have any siblings, right?" he asked.

I shook my head. "Do you?"

"Used to. An older brother." He took a big swig, and I copied him.

Over the next hour and a half, we drank and drank, and unprompted, he talked and talked, gazing at the blank wall to my left with a fond smile on his face most of the time as if he were watching the memories he recalled play out on an invisible screen, a screen privy to his eyes only.

He told me how he and his older brother Sam had spent most of their afternoons and evenings at a pond by their farmhouse. He told me about the giant, one-eyed catfish they'd caught and cooked over a fire on the bank, how Sam had convinced their friend Shelly to meet them there and give them both blowjobs in the tall grass, and how Sam had smuggled one of their dad's whiskey bottles out of the house and given Luther his first taste of liquor under the shade of a giant willow tree , causing him to puke his guts out in the water, bringing a gang of catfish to the surface to feed on his partially digested peas and bread.

He looked away from the wall and at me only when he recalled Sam's death. One summer afternoon, Sam had jumped off one of the giant willow's branches that dangled over the water—the same one he and Luther had jumped off of a hundred times—and hit his head on a rock and drowned. Luther had dived into the pond, dragged his brother to the bank, and ran home for help. But when he returned with his dad, Sam was dead.

A long silence spooled out after he finished that story. When I broke it by asking him where he'd grown up, he walked into the kitchen, refilled both our glasses with whiskey, came back, and changed the subject.

Staring at the wall again, he told me about a boy named John who lived on a farm near his family's and had constantly picked on him, partly because he was an easy target, small and perpetually sick, but also because his mother was known in the community as a former whore. One day Sam had convinced Luther to stand up to John, and Luther had told John to shut up, that his mom had been baptized and "born again," but John had spat in his face and called him "whore child" like always. The day after, Sam and Luther cornered John in his cornfield and beat the shit out of him with sticks as fat as baseball bats, spitting on his bloody face and hollering insults at him as he lay moaning in the dirt.

He also told me about his first girlfriend, Dolly. At thirteen he'd been knee-deep in love with her. He'd written her poems, picked her wild flowers and left them on her porch at night, made out with her and fingered her under The Monster, but then one day on his way to her house, he saw her fucking Jack Clawson on a blanket in the field behind her barn. Jack— the only fourteen-year-old in the county with chest hair and a beard— was on top, pounding her, but without Sam by his side, he didn't have the courage to confront them. Dolly broke up with Luther two days later and according to him, went on to fuck every boy he knew over the next few years. She died shortly after her eighteenth birthday, about a month after Sam. Luther didn't say exactly how, but based on the Luther I knew, I had a good guess.

By the time Luther finished talking, the whiskey had dulled my senses and slowed my thought process quite a bit, but not enough that I overlooked the contrast between his apparent age and dated stories. By his physical appearance, I figured he could be much older than thirty, possibly a young forty, but he talked as though he grew up in the 1800s. His stories had no TVs, no vehicles, no phones, no computers.

I was staring at the floor, struggling to rationalize the contrast, debating whether I should mention it or not, whether he'd give me an answer or not, when he asked me a question. "Do you think Brianne would ever cheat on you?"

I looked at him. He was still staring at the wall with a faraway look in his eyes. "No," I said. "She's not the type."

"What would you do if she did?"

"I don't know."

He smirked, finished his drink, and stood. "Well, I'm going to get some sleep. You should, too. I have something important to show you in the morning."

I followed him downstairs, went to my room, and shut the door. I flopped onto the bed without undressing, brushing my teeth, or calling Brianne. I'd texted her after the plane had landed and she'd texted back twice, asking me to call her later. As I lay in the darkness drifting off, I wondered what she was doing, what I would do if she cheated on me, if she ever wanted to, if she already had. With who? She'd forgiven me when I'd drunk-fucked that Mexican girl after a fight early in our relationship. I honestly didn't know if I could do the same.

Luther shook me awake at 4AM. I shot upright and didn't remember where I was or who he was for a moment. He turned on the lamp on the bedside table. He had his blue coat and ski pants on again.

Luther. Colorado. Shit.

"Grab your coat and let's go," he ordered.

Still buzzed and a bit disoriented, I did as instructed and followed him to the front door where he handed me a flashlight.

"Keep up," he said, and led me out into the darkness.

The frigid air stung my exposed skin. I pulled my hood up over my lucky Rangers cap, turned on the flashlight, shoved my free hand in my pocket, and mindlessly followed him.

We moved downhill into the large valley, weaving through the blanket of conifers, dodging drop-offs and trees and thick thorny brush areas. We moved at a brisk pace, and I had to call out for Luther a couple of times when I lost sight of him. I'm not sure exactly how far we'd walked by the time we came to the clearing, but I figure it was a couple of miles.

The clearing was covered in a thin film of snow, a crescent moon directly overhead shining bright. When I stopped next to Luther, I tucked the flashlight under my arm, and blew into my cupped hands to warm them. The fingers on my right hand, my nose, and cheeks were numb. Luther stared toward the treeline at the opposite end of the clearing, about twenty-five yards away.

"What are we looking at?" I asked.

He glanced at me, back at the tree line, then marched to the center of the clearing. As I followed him, a muffled scream shot across the night air. I stopped mid-stride and shined my flashlight beam at the back of Luther's head. He faced me and pointed to my left, the direction the scream had come from. "Shine your light over there."

I hesitated before aiming the flashlight that direction. The beam fell on a naked man who was tied to a dead tree trunk about fifteen yards away. A rope wrapped around his chest, another around his upper thighs, anchoring him to the tree. A red cloth was stuffed in his mouth. His large gut hung low, covering most of his privates. Even at that distance, I could see his eyes were wild-wide. Horrified. Just like the girl in the sack in Randy's truck. He didn't appear to be injured. A few blue jays were hopping around on the ground in front of him. I slowly moved the light back to Luther, trembling so bad my teeth were chattering.

"This guy invested in a company with me," he said, his accusatory finger aimed at the man. "And he has lived twenty luxurious years because of it. He could've lived twenty more, but he decided to do something stupid." He glanced at the guy, back at me. "I've already taken care of the person he blabbed to, but I brought him here so you could see firsthand how serious the consequences will be if you ever break our agreement. I like you, Seth, I really do, and I don't want you getting sloppy like this guy did...like Randy did. This is for your own good. For your family's good. Keep your light on me."

He dashed toward the man in a blur, crossing the distance in a blink. Then he repeatedly tapped the man's chest, yelling words I couldn't make out. The man shook his head vigorously, seemingly trying to scream and plead with Luther with his eyes. I initially wanted to run over to Luther and yell "stop" or "don't," to beg him to let the man at least speak. I even took a few steps forward. But then I thought better of it and stopped. I thought of Brianne and Sera and what the consequences would be of interfering.

My flashlight beam shook as Luther continued jabbing the man in the chest with a stiff finger. Ten or twenty blue jays were crowded around his feet now, some occasionally fluttering a few feet up into the air, chirping with excitement.

Luther smashed the man's face sideways into the trunk and leaned in close enough to kiss his neck. The bird noise grew louder, their fluttering chaotic. Luther's head twitched and jerked. I struggled to hold the light steady. When Luther twisted away from the man, I nearly dropped the flashlight. He had blood all over his face and the chest of his blue coat. The man had a jagged, gaping wound on his neck, blood gushing from the wound in fat spurts, running down his chest and leg like a raging river, mixing with the piss drizzling from his crotch. He wasn't dead yet. His eyes were pregnant with pain. His mouth silently opened and closed a few times as if he were biting chunks off an invisible apple.

Lightheaded, I fell to a knee. I ducked my head and lowered the flashlight for a terrifying second. But when I heard the bird's wing's flapping intensify, I looked up and moved the flashlight toward them. They were all air-born, a cloud of smudged blue hovering around Luther and the man. I moved the flashlight away, angled my eyes down. As I placed my hand on my head, fighting an urge to collapse, to puke, to scream, Luther suddenly appeared at my side and grabbed my wrist. A feeling of pure terror, drowning terror, deathly terror, assaulted me, stifled my breathing. "Do you understand the stakes?" he whispered. "Do you see my power?"

His hot breath brought gooseflesh to my cold ear. I understood all right. Crystal clear. I tried to nod, but I'm not sure if I did.

"Get out of here," he whispered, removing his hand. "I'll be in touch." Then, in a blur, he dashed back toward the tree and the birds and the man.

I snuck one last glance at them before bolting to the cabin. Luther was directly in front of the man, with his head tilted sideways—the nucleus in an atom of blue birds. Some of the birds were perched on the dead man's head and shoulders, pecking at the blood on his neck. A few others were on the ground, pecking at the pool of blood between his legs.

Swinging the flashlight like a baton, I sprinted uphill toward the cabin as fast as I could. By the time I reached the front porch, I was heaving, struggling to pull enough oxygen from the thin air to keep from fainting. My face was scraped from pushing through crowds of conifers, my pants torn and bloodied from several trips and falls. The palms of my hands were scraped from latching onto jagged branches when I'd lost my balance and gravity tried to force me downhill.

I ran inside the cabin, grabbed my bag, phone, and rental car keys, then ran to the Tahoe and sped away. I wasn't sure how to navigate the dirt roads to reach the highway, but I didn't care. I had to get away. Far away. Anywhere away.

Luther had predicted my fleeing and directional confusion

and had prepared a solution. At each fork in the dirt road, a blue jay was waiting in a nearby tree. When my headlights lit a fork and I slowed, the bird would swoop down and fly at windshield-level down one of the paths. Although terrified and frazzled, I knew to follow them. When my tires hit the highway that led me to back to Denver, I saw the last bird I would see until I arrived back in Mercy.

In the weeks that followed, the naked man visited me in my sleep often. Damn near every night. Every time he'd rip free of the ropes binding him to the tree and rush me with vengeance in his eyes, bleeding from the neck, a trail of squawking blue jays in his wake. He'd tackle me, straddle me, jam his finger in my chest, and scream, "Why didn't you help? Why? Why? Why?" As the repeated "why?" grew louder and louder, more and more of his spit and blood landed on my face, in my eyes, in my screaming mouth.

Brianne took notice of the nightmares, the sweating and tossing and turning, but I told her the dreams were about my mom. That Mom was lost somewhere in Lummorville, and I couldn't find her. I told Brianne I probably kept having the dream because Mom's birthday was approaching, and she bought it, hook, line, and sinker. She always had a soft spot for my mom and Lummorville.

Sorry, Bri.

Eleven

Notes and Bodies

The five-day trip to D.C. was a success. Ryan and one of Sera's friends came with us. We stayed in a fancy hotel with an indoor swimming pool and ordered expensive room service every night. We visited the White House, Smithsonian, and Lincoln Memorial, and scored tickets to a Redskins/Cowboys game on Thanksgiving Day. We returned to Mercy with more than enough souvenirs, pictures, and memories. Unfortunately, many of my memories were tainted by the blue jays that followed us around. I noticed them nearly everywhere we went, but no one else did.

In Mercy, the blue jays kept a vigilant eye on me as well. They built a nest in the tree behind our duplex, one in my dad's front yard elm, and daily visited the new construction site in southeast Mercy where we'd started a government housing complex project.

But Luther didn't contact me again until three months after the Colorado trip, the weekend Sera turned thirteen.

I had taken her and two of her friends to the mall so she could spend her birthday money ($300—six times the amount from the previous year). While they shopped, I ate a slice of pizza in the Food Court, had a lengthy discussion with Dan about an upcoming project, walked around the mall a couple of times, bought Brianne the Neil Finn CD she'd hinted at wanting, then met the girls in front of the dollar theater at 9PM as planned. The girls were looking at the movie posters, talking, holding their bags of new clothes.

"So what movie do you guys want to see?" I asked.

"The one with Matthew McConaughey," Sera said. She glanced at the other girls and they giddily agreed.

"I think I'll sit this one out," I said. "McConaughey's not my type."

Sera's friends giggled. She punched me in the arm. Just like Brianne had taught her. "Do you have enough money for drinks and food and everything?" I asked.

"Yeah," Sera said. "We have plenty."

"All right. I'll meet you guys here when the show is over. Promise me you won't go anywhere else or talk to any creepy older guys in there."

Sera playfully rolled her eyes. "I promise. What are you gonna do?"

"I don't know. I need to call Brianne real quick then I might come back and check out the Jason Bourne flick or something." I gestured at her bags. "You want me to take those for you?"

"Sure." Sera handed over her bags, and I offered to take the other two girl's bags as well and they passed them to me. Then Sera pecked me on the cheek, took one of her friends by the hand, and they hurried to the ticket booth.

I waited while they purchased tickets and drinks and popcorn, waved to Sera, and headed to my truck.

I saw the note under the Chevy's wiper blade from ten cars away and my muscles tensed. I stopped mid-stride, wanting to turn around and march back into the mall and pretend I hadn't seen it. But I continued to the truck, set the girl's bags in the cab, and took the note off the windshield. As I read it, a blue jay landed on the hood.

Thanks for helping out.

The bird hopped closer to me, its nails clicking on the hood. I passed it the note but didn't bother watching it fly away. I didn't bother checking the bed for the burlap sack, either. I knew it was there. I knew what I had to do. I checked the time on my cell phone. I had two hours until the girl's show would end, enough time if I hurried. I didn't want the girls in the truck with the corpse.

I drove to the southeast side of town and buried the sack in the corner of the soon-to-be parking lot of the government housing project without incident. I had to use a hand shovel this time because unlike West Hill, the new site wasn't secluded enough for me to use the Bobcat without recognition; a busy Popeye's Chicken was a block away.

As I feverishly scooped soil, I tried to drive my thoughts in any direction other than toward the corpse in the sack with thin shoulders and wide hips. I thought about how what I was doing was helping everyone I loved, making them happy, giving them opportunities and vacations and security. I thought about how I didn't have a choice, how I couldn't change the fate of whoever was in that sack anyway. How I *could* change the fate of my loved one's lives by digging the hole and keeping my mouth shut. I thought about Brianne's excited squee when I'd mentioned maybe buying her a new car. About Sera's joy at having a closet full of new clothes, a new dresser, new jewelry. About Ryan's relief at having a large chunk of his debt paid off. But by the time I was smoothing the soil on top of the hole my thoughts had drifted to the big-hipped woman in the sack. How she may have died. What her last thought on Earth was. What her eyes looked like inside there.

After I picked up the girls and we were on our way home, it occurred to me that I hadn't washed the Chevy since I'd met Luther, since he'd been in the cab, right where Sera was sitting and chatting about Matthew McConaughey's abs with her friends. The idea of Sera being that close to Luther sickened me. The next morning, I scrubbed the entire thing, inside and out. Brianne and Sera both offered to help, but I refused their offers.

I washed it the night of or day after every burial from then on.

A month later I received a note that simply read *Delivery*. I found it one morning before work and therefore had to keep the corpse in my truck all day—one of the longest days of my life.

The new grunt workers Dan had hired for the government housing project made quite a few mistakes that day because I watched my truck more than I watched them. I spent my morning break, lunch hour, and afternoon break pacing around my truck, pretending to be on the phone with Brianne, shooing away anyone who came close.

After work, I drove straight home, parked in front of the carport, plopped down in one of the lawn chairs, and stared at the bed until the sun fell below the horizon. Brianne came out a couple of times and asked if I was all right, and I told her I was stressed about work and missing Randy. Which wasn't an absolute lie. I was stressed about work. Just a different type of work. And I did miss Randy. Because if he were still around, my burden wouldn't have...it doesn't matter. That's not fair. It wasn't his fault.

For safe measure, I checked the Chevy's lights and blinkers and tags before driving to the government housing site. We had one building left to complete and were supposed to lay a cement sidewalk with a wheelchair ramp in front of it the following morning. I parked next to the cement truck, Bobcat, and front loader, then dug the hole in the leveled soil where the ramp would go and went to retrieve the sack.

It was twice as heavy as the previous ones. One-hundred-forty pounds or more. And it felt different. The way it balled-up in the bottom of the burlap. The way it shifted as I walked. Like pieces of a jigsaw puzzle trying to squirm their way into the right slot, to make a coherent picture. I especially didn't like the way it felt when it brushed against my thigh and shin. No matter how hard I tried to hold the sack away from my body I felt the brushing, the shifting, which conjured horrible images in my mind of tiny babies squashed together inside, wide-eyed as the girl I'd found in Randy's truck, fighting for comfortable position. The image was accompanied by a sinister whisper in my head, Luther's hiss: "Babies. Babies. Babies. You're burying tiny little babies. Ha, ha, ha."

I closed my eyes when I reached the hole, and against my better judgment, I decided to dump out the contents of the bag rather than just drop it in. I couldn't help it. I had to see what was inside. I had to know.

A relieved sigh burst through my clenched lips when I shone my keychain light down in the hole and saw a heap of cats and dogs and large rats instead of babies. They were all eyeless and poked with tiny bird-beak-size peck holes, but at least they weren't babies. I tossed the sack over the animals, and filled and smoothed the hole faster than I had any other hole in my entire life.

It wasn't until later that night while I lay in bed, slipping in and out of a mild sleep, that my imagination ran wild with bird-feast images. They weren't feasting on cats and dogs and rats, though. They were feasting on babies. I didn't sleep well that night. Or for weeks after.

I saw the next note on the Chevy when I peeked out the front window after dinner the day before Valentine's Day. I didn't even read it. I glanced in the cab, saw the sack, then simply held the note in the air. A few seconds later, a blue jay snatched it and carried it away. After telling Brianne I thought I'd accidentally left the keys in the ignition of the Bobcat and needed to go check, I left.

I parked across the street from Crocket Elementary. The new state-of-the-art school was located west of the West Hill neighborhood, close to the pond where the bird bandits had lived, had been built by Washer Construction over the fall and winter. But when vandalism claims on their equipment and contract disputes with the city halted the finishing of the sidewalks and playground area, we stepped in. We'd leveled a large rectangular patch of land for a basketball court the day before.

I walked around to the back of the school, shoved my hands deep in my pockets, and examined the area. The closest inhabited houses were two city blocks away. No street lights had been erected above the roads yet in front of the school yet.

The thought of burying the burlap sack in a spot where kids would be laughing and playing unnerved me, but I didn't have a choice. And, selfishly, I just wanted to get it done and get home. As I took slow measured breaths to still myself for the job at hand, I heard footsteps behind me. Before I could spin around, a flashlight beam hit my back, casting my long silhouette out onto the freshly leveled dirt.

"Put your hands in the air," a man ordered.

I obeyed, and slowly turned toward the voice. A uniformed cop held the flashlight head-high, had his other hand at his waist, hovering above his gun like a gunfighter awaiting the signal to draw. He was tall and stalky, middle-aged with pock marks on his cheeks and thin wire-rim glasses covering his eyes. I didn't recognize him. "What are you doing out here?" he asked.

Despite the cold temperature, sweat beaded up on my forehead beneath my lucky Rangers cap. "I work out here, sir." My voice cracked with the "sir."

"What are you doing out here this late?"

I forced a dry swallow, tried to gather enough spit to speak with confidence. "Just making sure we have everything ready for tomorrow's cement pouring. We're putting in the basketball court." A beat. "And to make sure nothing's happened to any of our supplies or trucks. After the vandalism that happened to Washer's stuff, you know?"

He moved the light away from my face and walked toward me. "Do you have any ID?"

"Yes, sir," I said, pulling my wallet out of my back pocket. I handed him my driver's license, and he scrutinized it with his flashlight.

"Is that your Chevy over there?" He gestured toward my truck with his flashlight. His cruiser was parked behind it with its headlights on. I nodded.

"What construction company do you work for?"

"Howe's Construction. Dan Howe's company."

"Worked there long?"

"Twelve years," I said, trying to sound proud about the length.

"Do you have any guns or weapons on you or in your truck?"

"No, sir." *Just a dead body.* With the thought came the realization that a blue jay was watching, perched on a pile of bricks stacked behind the officer.

"I'm going to pat you down real quick, anyway. For my safety." He gently frisked me, patting down my pant and coat pockets.

"It's a little cold out to be sweating, isn't it?" he asked, eyeing my face.

I wiped the sweat away with my sleeve. "Just a nervous reaction I guess. You scared the shit out of me."

He held my gaze for a moment, reading my lie as easy as a *Dick and Jane* book, or so I thought. He gestured toward our vehicles. "Let's walk over there so I can run your license for warrants."

He followed me to my truck and told me to stand by the tailgate, in the cruiser's headlights. As he sat in his driver's seat and pulled up my arrest record, my eyes slid over everything in the bed of my truck besides the burlap sack by the back window. I purposefully didn't look at that, paranoid that acknowledging it with my eyes would reveal its contents. I lowered my head, stooped, and rested it on the tailgate. What if he does find it? I thought. What if I go to jail? What would I say? I jerked my head up when a blue jay landed on top of the cab. What am I going to do? I thought at the bird. If I get caught what will Luther do to me? To Sera? To Brianne? What will they think? The questions and consequences and time it was taking the officer to finish checking my license all seemed endless. Torturous. My sweat had doubled in volume and stink.

"Here you go," the officer said, holding my license out for me when he finally came back.

I put it in my wallet as he bounced his flashlight around the bed of my truck. The shovels, buckets, tools, wood, sheet rock. Burlap sack. Every time it crossed the sack, my heart hiccupped. When he finished, he walked to the cab and shown the beam through the open window, jiggled it around a bit, then came back to me. I don't think he noticed the bird staring down at him like a tiny gargoyle. "You had anything to drink tonight?" he asked.

He must've seen the two DWI arrests on my record. One fourteen years earlier, the other, two months after Esperanza died. "No, sir," I replied, silently thanking God that I hadn't met up with Ryan and the guys at Wizzards after work like I'd initially planned. A call from Brianne asking me to stop by the store for some flour had derailed those plans.

He inhaled deeply up his nose as I answered. A deliberate search for alcohol on my breath. "I understand you guys don't want anyone damaging your trucks, but for your own safety I'd suggest that you don't come out here this late at night. We are sending patrol cars out here every couple of hours to check on the place."

I nodded. "Yes, sir. I was just nervous, you know? Deadlines?"

"I hear you," he said, and gave a curt farewell head nod. "Have a good night."

"You, too," I said, and then got in my truck. Not until I sat down did I realize my legs and hands were shaking. I started my truck, turned on the headlights, took a series of deep breaths, and waited for the cruiser to pull away first.

After filling up with gas at a nearby Toot 'n Totum, the same one the officer had coincidentally stopped at, I turned off my phone so no one would be able to reach me and drove forty-five miles northeast of Mercy.

Plemons was out in the middle of nowhere, thirty miles from any modern city. In the late eighteen and early nineteen hundreds it had been a lively pioneer town. Bank. Post office. Jail. The works. But like many original plains towns, it had been abandoned after a measles outbreak killed most of the children. A small gravesite is all that's left of it now. Cattle ranchers and oil companies own the land. And they've blocked off or bulldozed the old roads that led to the town to discourage visitors. Most people, including myself, probably couldn't find the actual town site, but anyone could find the metal, one-way Plemons Bridge that crossed the Canadian River headed that direction. Oil pump repairmen, dirt bikers, and hunters frequented the dirt roads and trails that crisscrossed the dry riverbed beneath the bridge, and teens were regularly busted there, using old oil pumps as gathering points for keg parties. That's how I originally learned of the area—high school keg parties.

After crossing the bridge, I parked in a copse of mesquite trees and made my way down to the dry river bed's edge with the burlap sack and a shovel. The soil was sandy and easy to maneuver. I dug as fast and as quietly as I could, and it didn't take long to complete the job.

I didn't notice any of Luther's birds until I crossed the bridge afterwards. Six or seven of them were lining the metal railing on the driver's side. Their heads swiveled to follow me as I passed, like motion-detector cameras.

Twelve

Breaking News

I hired a part-time home assistant for Dad in spring. Lucy Jordan was her name. She was a twenty-six-year-old, doe-eyed nurse who worked for The Mercy Home Nursing Alliance. She was tough as nails, inside and out. Just the type of person Dad needed to keep him in line. Her husband had died in Afghanistan a year earlier—road side bomb one month into his first tour—leaving her a five-year-old son to care for.

She came to Dad's house five days a week, Monday through Friday, five hours a day, sometimes in the afternoon, sometimes morning, sometimes night. She helped him clean, organize his meals and medications, drove him to the store and doctor appointments, and did memory exercises with him every day. She and Dr. Hale said that the simple mental exercises along with his medication could help slow his dementia. When I arrived at his home one Sunday to eat dinner and play Texas Rummy with him and Brenda, Lucy was just leaving. I stopped on the front porch and asked how Dad was today.

She flashed a tired PR smile. "He's good. He's got a lot of energy so we did some yard work in the back, and then I helped him and Brenda cook dinner for you guys. Where's Brianne and Sera? Brenda said they were coming."

I checked the time on my cell phone. "Brianne just got off work. She's going to pick up Sera from a friend's house and then they'll be here."

"Good, good," she said. "Well, I have to go to my mom's house and pick up Jimmy so I better get."

Jimmy was her five-year-old son. "All right. Have a...oh, wait. I almost forgot." I fished five twenty-dollar bills from my pocket and held them out for her. "Here you go."

She looked at the money but didn't take it. "I've told you before that you don't have to tip me, Mr. Fow—I mean, Seth."

"I know. I want to."

Her tired smile and her chocolate eyes perked up, and she took the money. "Thank you."

"You're welcome. Have a good one."

Shortly after Lucy drove off, Brianne and Sera pulled up in Brianne's whiny, white Taurus that had a mismatched tan fender and a glued-on driver's side mirror. We'd bought the car eight years earlier when Brianne landed a job at Golden Corral and had pumped no less than five hundred bucks into it every year to keep it afloat. I met them on the sidewalk, hugged them, and we all went inside.

Dad was in his recliner watching a John Wayne flick. Brenda was adding the extension to the dining table so everyone could sit together. Brianne rushed to help her while Sera and I greeted Dad, who seemed mentally lucid and energetic like Lucy had said. Which was good. Sera knew her Papa had bad days when he didn't know his asshole from a hole in the ground, and that he sometimes cussed at me and became violent for no apparent reason, I just didn't want her to see those ugly moments with her own eyes. I wanted her to remember my dad as the quirky old man who pulled small treasures out of her ear, told tasteless jokes, and teased her about the springiness of her curly hair.

For dinner, Lucy, Brenda, and Dad had made a stroganoff casserole, rolls, green beans, and sweet tea. Brownies for dessert. For an hour we ate and engaged in small talk. We chatted about Brenda's homegrown tomatoes and green beans, Sera's "hideous" math teacher whose breath smelled of cigarettes and beard regularly had powdered donut crumbs stuck in it, Brianne's sixteen-year-old co-worker who was pregnant for the second time, and my latest job—building a storage facility in western Mercy so the rich had more space to store their toys.

After dinner, Brianne and I cleared the table and cleaned up the kitchen while Sera cut the brownies and Brenda and

Dad prepared the table for the card game, finding the deck of cards and pencil and paper needed to keep score. Playing Texas Rummy had been a ritual at all my mom's family's holiday gatherings when I was a kid. She'd taught me and Dad how to play and I'd taught Brianne, Ryan, and Sera. The four of us had spent countless hours playing under our carport on warm summer evenings, and we played an annual Christmas Eve game every year. Good memories.

We laughed and played until almost ten o'clock. Sera came out on top, earning the grand prize customarily taped to the center of the table—twenty bucks. Which used to be five in less prosperous times. Dad ribbed her, accused her of cheating and demanded she fork over the twenty. She was the score keeper and no one had verified her math, he claimed. She gave him a sassy, ornery look—a look that her mom had given me numerous times—and told him to prove it.

Brenda hugged everyone and went home to let her Chihuahua Fruity out to pee. Dad sat down in his recliner and cranked up the volume on the news. After we shrunk the table back into a small square, Brianne and I joined Sera on the couch. We watched the weather and listened to Dad chide the weatherman, calling him a "smarmy liar," claiming flipping a coin would give the same results as all their fancy gadgetry. During the next commercial break, Brianne gave me her *let's-go* look.

Sera hugged Dad first, and he pulled a five-dollar bill out of her ear. Brianne hugged him next, then I shook his hand and told him I'd call him tomorrow. We were headed out the door when Channel 10 news anchor Michelle Farmer, a skinny blonde-haired girl with blue eyes and thick black glasses, appeared on the television screen and said something that shattered the peaceful sensation I'd had the entire evening. I hadn't thought of Luther or the birds once since we'd arrived.

"In the last ten months, four alleged prostitutes who frequented Mercy Boulevard have been reported missing," Michelle said, her words like a snake bite to my neck. I froze with my hand on the doorknob and stared at the TV as Brianne and Sera continued chatting on their way to the Taurus.

"Although many of the alleged Boulevard prostitutes are transients and often leave town unannounced, the news is still very disconcerting to the friends and families of the missing," Michelle continued. "Especially Amber Powell's. She was the only one of the four women who was a lifelong Mercy resident, and her sister is the person who contacted us for help finding her sister."

The screen cut to a small woman with light brown hair and hazel eyes who looked oddly familiar. She held a flyer in front her chest. Below the name rendered in all capitals—AMBER POWELL—was a picture of a pretty girl who appeared to be a teenager. I inched toward the TV. Her hair was shorter and styled with bangs, and her eyes were squinty from the giant smile on her face, but it was her. The girl in the sack in back of Randy's truck. The girl I'd called the police about. That's why the sister looked familiar. The family resemblance. Her sister (Darcy Powell according to the label on the bottom of the screen) told Michelle Farmer that she last talked to Amber last summer. She admitted Amber was a prostitute and struggled with drug addiction, but she claimed Amber would never go this long without contacting her. Or just up and leave town like the police suggested. They were best friends. Shared an apartment. "Something bad has happened to her, I know it. And somebody out there knows what. Please help me find my sister." Her plea brought tears to her eyes and an ache to my chest.

The screen cut back to the live studio where Michelle Farmer said, "I also spoke with Detective Morrell of the Mercy Police Department this afternoon."

Morrell was standing slumped-shouldered in front of the police building downtown. He wore a '70s-style brown suit and looked like he'd dipped his hair in a vat of oil, making the comb trails appear deep as ravines. I hadn't spoken to him about Randy in more than six months. "We are giving the disappearances of Amber Powell, C.C. Jackson, Staci Umbarger, and J'Qaunda Jones the due attention they deserve. We take their family's and friend's reports seriously and are taking all actions necessary to find these women. Unfortunately, missing person cases involving women who are allegedly involved in prostitution are often the hardest to solve. They tend to move around and change appearances frequently."

"What would you say to any of the women if they're watching?" Michelle asked.

Morrell's droopy eyes slid to the camera. *To me.* "I'd tell them that their family and friends are worried, and I'd ask them to please contact just one person so we'll know they're okay. That's all we want."

The honk of Brianne's Taurus pulled my eyes away from the TV as Michelle Farmer began giving statistics about missing women in Texas and the entire United States. I glanced out the front door and saw them pulling away from the curb, Sera waving from the passenger seat. I waved back, then turned to Dad. He was staring at the TV, at a blaring commercial about foundation repair. I told him "bye" again, made sure the door was locked, then hurried to my truck.

I sat there for a long while, staring at the blue jay in Dad's elm tree. Learning Amber Powell's name, seeing her face— her vibrant smiling face— was like a punch to the gut. Like a spotlight of reality cast on my actions. Before, she'd just been a random woman, a nameless pair of eyes. *A sex-doll.* But now she was a young prostitute from Mercy with addiction problems and a heart-broken sister. If I had just taken her out of Randy's truck that night, right then and there, and had the cojones to make him face the music, everything would be different. She'd still be dead, sure, but her sister would know where she was. And I wouldn't be in the position I was...and on and on.

For about the hundredth time, regret pummeled me as I thought of all the things I could've done different. Done better. But as I stared at that blue jay staring at me, deep down I knew that things wouldn't have been better-different. Just different.

First off, I would've been dead. Perhaps tied to a tree and slaughtered to prove a point to some other poor soul. Luther would've found someone else to be his puppet, his utensil, his temporary plaything. And the killings definitely would've continued. If not in Mercy then somewhere else. Because Luther would've gone on doing what Luther does. And God knows what would've happened to Brianne and Sera. And Dad.

Maybe nothing. But maybe more than I want my imagination to guess at. Besides, if I allow myself a moment of selfishness, Dad wouldn't have had the extra help. Esperanza wouldn't have a proper tombstone. Brianne's and Ryan's mom wouldn't have a bed and the medicine she needed. Lucy wouldn't have had a job with massive tips to help with her son Jimmy. Our neighbors wouldn't have had the new set of tires on their Beretta—tires that kept them from losing their jobs and becoming homeless. Ryan wouldn't have been able to open his first savings account. Brianne wouldn't have had a sparkle in her eyes when she talked about having enough of a financial cushion to maybe, possibly, have a baby of her own. And Sera wouldn't have had everything a young girl needs in today's world in order to maximize her opportunities, both socially and economically.

When I finally left my dad's house, I drove to Wizzards, sat in the same booth I'd sat in the night I met Luther, and drank until my conscience stopped being able to offer up questions. Then I drank more. Until I fully drowned the feeling of regret swimming in my chest.

Thirteen

A Fit Proposal and Wedding

Shortly after Brianne's shift started one sunny summer afternoon, Ryan dropped me and Sera off behind the Corral next
to the dumpsters. Brianne and the other Golden Corral employ-
ees parked behind the restaurant. Using a spare of set of keys,
we took Brianne's Taurus to the Honda dealership downtown
and traded it (I got a whopping three hundred bucks for it)
toward a silver Honda Fit.

Brianne had been coveting the Fits for a while. Every time
we'd pass the lot she'd comment on how cute and spunky
they were, or how good of gas mileage they got compared to
her Taurus, or how the hatch back would be perfect for when
she helped deliver the Golden Corral's catering. She wanted
one, bad, but having been raised in a way that didn't allow
personal purchases for anything other than necessities, never
for anything that cost more than five or ten dollars at that, she
never would've asked for one outright. Old habits die hard. So
I bought it for her.

And since I'd taken such a big step, big in our world anyway,
I decided to take one more and ask her to marry me.

Beginning with the conversation we'd had the first night I
laid eyes on her at Wizzards and bought her a couple of drinks,
we'd both always expressed a lack of interest in marriage. She
never actually admitted it, but I attributed her lack of interest
to the various failed marriages she and Ryan had watched her
mother endure. Cecilia Collier had been married five times
and none of those guys were Brianne's or Ryan's fathers.

Husbands number one, three, and four were mooching drunks with aggressive tempers who hit their mom regularly (not that she didn't occasionally throw the first punch). Number three actually beat her bad enough to put her in the hospital a couple of times. Husband two turned out to be gay—she caught him sucking a neighbor's dick in the garage one afternoon—and husband five was a flat-out pervert. "He'll fuck anything with a hole," Brianne's mom had once said. He'd even tried to poke Brianne one night while she slept in her panties and T-shirt on the couch when she was twelve. Her mom initially pressed charges on the guy, but later, just before the divorce, dropped them for some unknown reason.

My initial disinterest in marriage was because of Esperanza. At one time, I thought she was my "soul mate," my "one true love," and I honestly didn't see ever loving anyone that hard again. But I was wrong. Within six months of knowing Brianne, I loved her every bit as much as I had Esperanza and wanted to spend the rest of my life with her. Yet I continued with the marriage-doesn't-matter façade for years. We both did. Anytime Ryan or someone else asked, "When are you two gonna get hitched already?" we'd laugh it off as irrelevant. A piece of paper. A tax-thing. A waste of money we didn't have. We were committed to one another with our hearts and that's all that mattered. But I could tell by the look in Brianne's eyes, by the hesitation of her response, a hesitation that grew longer every time the issue arose, that she'd turned a corner. She wanted to get married.

Five minutes before Brianne's lunch break, Sera and I placed the engagement ring I'd bought a few weeks earlier on the Fit's key ring, put the key in the ignition, then hid with Ryan behind the dumpsters.

As Brianne walked out the back door and headed to her Taurus for her customary smoke, my stomach danced with excitement. I covered Sera's mouth to stifle her giggling when Brianne realized her Taurus was missing. Brianne stopped and her mouth dropped open. She slammed her hands onto her hips, threw her head back, and yelled, "Goddammit!" As she lowered her head and noticed the Fit, the dealer tags, her expression changed from anger to confusion. I took my hand off Sera's mouth, and told her and Ryan, "Let's go."

Crouched low, we crept out from behind the dumpster and made our way to the back of the Fit. Then on the count of three, we jumped up and yelled, "Surprise!"

Brianne's eyes widened in startled shock, but she didn't move or say anything. Sera rushed over, grabbed her by the hand, and led her to the Fit. Ryan slapped my back, we high-fived, and followed them.

"Get in," Sera told Brianne, opening the driver's door. "Check it out." Sera peered at me as Brianne sat down, and I could practically see our ring-secret leaking from her eyes. I winked at her and then bent forward, putting my hands on my knees so I could see Brianne. "What do you think?" I asked.

Brianne craned her neck, taking in the car's interior. She sighed, put her hands on the wheel, and leaned back. "It's great," she said. "Perfect." She cut her eyes at me. "You didn't have to do this. You should've gotten yourself a truck."

"You deserve it more than I do," I said. And she did.

Sera poked her head under my arm. "Start it up," she said.

When Brianne reached toward the ignition, I knelt. She noticed the ring before she turned the key and looked at me, at the ring, at me. Sera made a girly squeaky noise and threw her hand over her own mouth. Brianne took the key out of the ignition, examined the ring, looked at me again, now with tears forming in her eyes. I'd only seen Brianne cry a handful of times in our years together and never from happiness. Knowing she was truly moved by the ring, I welled up, too.

"I know we always said it didn't matter if we ever got officially married, but I want to," I said. "I want to share a name with you. Will you marry me?"

A soft chirp-laugh popped out of her mouth, and she hugged me. "Of course I will."

She went inside and told her co-workers, showed them the ring, and her boss let her have the rest of the day off. Later that night, we had a celebratory pizza dinner, and after Ryan left and Sera fell asleep, Brianne and I snuck out to the Fit and properly broke it in, like we had the Taurus and the Chevy.

I hadn't noticed any birds at the Golden Corral, thank God, but of course they were there. Watching. Listening.

The next morning, I found a note on my truck's windshield that said *Congratulations*. I crumpled it up and tossed it out the window on my way to work. Although pleased to find it wasn't for another burial job, I hated being reminded that Luther was always lingering, watching, inspecting. Like some demented puppeteer constantly monitoring the durability of his puppet's strings.

Brianne and I weren't regular churchgoers. We took Sera to Christmas Eve and Easter services at the non-denominational church on 45th Street Esperanza had had her baptized in, but that was it. Brianne still wanted to have the wedding in a church, though. As a kid, she had walked Ryan to the Lutheran church down the street from their apartment for warmth in the winter, air conditioning in the summer, and free lunch the first Sunday of every month. She was grateful for the generosity of Pastor Dietz and the Lutheran congregation and wanted him to marry us, which was fine with me.

After applying for a marriage license at the downtown municipal building, we stopped by the Lutheran church because Brianne wanted me to see the inside and meet Pastor Dietz. She'd already phoned him, and he remembered her and Ryan and was delighted she wanted to get married in the "right way," in his church.

He was seventy-one-years old, short and fat and bald. He had warm, swollen hands that hinted at high blood pressure, rosacea on his cheeks that hinted he sipped the communion wine at home as well as at church, and soft, welcoming eyes that hinted at a caring heart. He asked us if we had accepted Jesus into our hearts as our Savior and we said "yes." Had we both been baptized? She had. I hadn't. Had we ever been married before? I told him about Esperanza. How long had we been living in sin? Ten plus years. Did we have any kids? Brianne explained Sera, and he seemed pleased with our dedication to her, and that she was baptized. He gave us a quick tour of the small sanctuary, which Brianne said hadn't changed a lick since she'd last been there nearly fifteen years earlier. A line of stained-glass windows with images depicting biblical scenes ran down the left wall, evenly spaced candle holders the brick wall on the right. The strip of carpet between the pews was blood red, the ceiling vaulted, the pulpit oak. We thanked him, told him we'd come back for a mandatory meeting with him the week before the wedding, then we left.

In the Fit on the way home, Brianne was quiet, her eyes serious and unflinching as she drove. When we stopped in front of our duplex, she killed the engine, and keeping her eyes aimed straight ahead, asked, "Are you sure you want to do this?"

It took a second for me to respond. "Yes. Of course."

"I think you're just doing it because you think I want it."

I didn't know what to say. I thought I'd showed the proper amount of enthusiasm about the wedding. I'd proposed, agreed to her church, and I thought I'd answered all Pastor Dietz's questions correctly, happily. I'd even squeezed her hand one solid time, a gesture we referred to as the Fowler Love Squeeze, before we walked into the sanctuary and again as we walked out.

"You seem distant lately," she said.

I scrunched my brow and shook my head soft and slow, hoping to imply that her statement had confused me.

"And not just since the proposal," she added. "It's been going on for a long time."

"What has?" I asked. My pulse quickened at the thought of her catching on to what I'd been doing. Questioning me about any missteps I may have made.

"You leave sometimes at night and don't come home until morning. You sleep on the couch sometimes. You've been drinking more." She pushed out a clutched breath. "You just don't seem fully engaged a lot of the time. With me. With Sera. In there with Pastor Dietz. Even when we were on vacation in D.C. You seem like you want to be somewhere else. With someone else. Like you're looking around waiting for something to change."

"I'm sorry if I've been a little distant lately, but I promise

I don't want to be with anyone else or anywhere else," I said. "You guys are my life." I went to my stock lie. "It's just that ever since Randy..." I almost said "died" but caught myself, swallowed hard. "You know. Work's been rough. Dan refuses to hire anyone else to help me run things and that puts a lot of added stress on me." I put my hand on her thigh. "It has nothing to do with you." She glanced at me. "I swear."

She seemed to buy it. Whether it was because deep down she wanted to or because I'd lied well enough, I didn't care. I just wanted the conversation to end. She nodded, pushed out a slow breath, and her eyes softened. "I know your work has been stressful this past year," she said. "And I know you miss Randy and that his disappearance and that girl's body freaked you out. And of course I know Dan is a major asshole. But you have to look at the positive. That investment you made is really opening things up for us. We have new opportunities now that we thought would always just be dreams."

I nodded. She was right. But she didn't know the cost of those opportunities. "I'm sorry," I said. "I promise I'll start trying harder."

"It's not tha—" She bit her lip, chewed on what she wanted to say for a moment. "Now that we have the extra income, I think you should seriously think about looking for a different job."

I shook my head. "I can't"

"Why not?" Her voice volume rose in frustration. "Why are you so devoted to Dan? He doesn't give a shit about you."

"I'm not devoted to him." *I'm devoted to Luther.* "It's a good job, and I'd have to start from scratch if I joined on with some other crew. I'm too old for that."

"You're only in your mid-forties. You could move up the ranks on any crew quick. They'd see how much you know right away."

I didn't bother responding. There was no point. We'd had this conversation many times before. She'd actually sent my résumé to two other construction companies five or six years back without my knowledge, resulting in huge arguments both times. She wasn't going to bend and neither was I. Especially now that my old job was tied to my new job.

To our "new opportunities".

To our lives.

I was changing into my tux when Ryan came into the small room that connected Pastor Dietz's office to the sanctuary—the room where Dietz and the acolyte robed before Sunday service. Ryan was already in his tux. His hair was slicked back in a tight ponytail, and he'd shaved the scrappy beard he'd attempted to grow. He reeked of cigarette smoke. I figured he'd been outside with Brianne. "How's she feeling?" I asked. She and Sera had left for Brenda's to get their hair done before I'd woken up.

"She's worried."

I was hoping he would've said "good" or "excited."

"About what? It's not like she doesn't know what she's jumping into. We've practically been married for ten years."

Ryan checked himself in the tall mirror on the wall, adjusted his jacket, then made eye contact with me. He looked nervous. "Don't tell her I told you this. I swore I wouldn't, and we both know how long and hard her grudges can run." I nodded. "She said she's worried about you. She thinks you might've met someone else. Or just don't love her anymore."

I shook my head. "Man, I can't believe she's bringing that up again with you. We talked about it already, and I told her I've just been stressed about work."

The tension in my voice caused Ryan to put his hands up in a submissive position. "Hey, don't get mad at me. I told her that. I told her there's no way you have another girl. I would know. I told her how Dan is expecting way too much from you ever since Randy disappeared, too." He paused, then turned and examined himself in the mirror again. "But I did tell her you've seemed more distant to me, too."

"What? How?"

"Well, for starters, you've been sitting alone in your truck at lunch instead of hanging out with us, and you don't come out for drinks with the guys after work anymore either." He glanced down, scanned the floor, looked up. "You haven't gone to a Sox game with me since early summer. Or come by the apartment to hang out and play Xbox like you sometimes used to."

"I know…but I…nothing's what it…whatever."

"It's no big deal, though," he said. "I know all that shit with Randy was disturbing, and all the pressure Dan puts on you is hard to deal with." He whipped a tiny spray can of breath freshener out of his pocket, spritzed his mouth, and faced me. "Let's not talk about this today. It's supposed to be a special day. A happy day." He popped me in the arm, and I jabbed him back, bringing a smile of approval to his face. "Bri will be fine anyway. She's just thinking about all that nonsense because that's what women do on their wedding day whether they've known the man ten days or ten years. They question every little fucking thing and freak out a little. Right?"

I gave a flimsy agreement-smile that Ryan took as genuine, but I had a sickening feeling in my gut. I sensed right then and there that a clock had started ticking, counting down to my unraveling, and there was no way to stop it. Brianne and Ryan's observations were spot on. Their concerns and questions directly on target. I wasn't sure how much longer I could effectively convince them nothing was wrong and conceal the turmoil stewing inside my heart and mind. I could only take long drives and spend time alone hiding in obscure bars for so long. They would eventually find out. They knew me too well, and I wasn't a good enough liar.

Ryan's close-set eyes widened as if he were suddenly struck by a marvelous idea. He flicked his index finger at me. "I'm going to my truck for a second. I'll be right back."

I walked over to the mirror to check out my tux. I'd never worn a proper suit much less a tuxedo. It felt as awkward as it looked. Out of place. Fake. Wrong. As I ran my hand over my fresh buzz cut, noticing the number of greys had significantly increased, the door to Pastor Dietz's office eased open and Luther slid in. He was dressed in a black Guayabera, black slacks, and black shiny shoes, and carried the scent of fresh lavender into the room with him.

"What are you doing here?" I asked, jerking my eyes left to right, left to right, as if someone might see him and know right away who or what he was, what our connection was, and all the horrible things we'd done.

"Chill out. I just came to congratulate you and give you this." He handed me an envelope stuffed with hundreds. "For your honeymoon. Or a nice present for Brianne. Whatever you want."

"I think you should go before anyone sees you," I said.

"Don't worry. No one will see me that I don't want to." He chuckled and put his hand on my shoulder. "You sure are high strung today, friend. You want me to remedy that for you? Take the edge off?" He tapped his fingers on my shoulder and winked at me.

I didn't want him there. I really didn't. I didn't want him invading my wedding. But he did. And since he was already there. And since deep down I knew he would *always* be there, until the day I died. And since I wanted to make sure Brianne saw that I was confident and calm and happy when she walked down the aisle. And since the sickening feeling I had in my gut was inching close to vomit level, I nodded and uttered, "Please."

Luther moved his hand from my shoulder to my exposed neck and I closed my eyes. "Anything for a friend," he said.

Like in the Colorado cabin, a warm soothing sensation flowed from his fingers into my skin. My muscles relaxed. My stomach settled. The tight knot of fretful thoughts in my mind untangled, dissolved, disappeared. I sighed and opened my eyes when he removed his hand. He had a satisfied sparkle in his eyes. Like a child who'd pleased his mother. He put his left hand in his pocket and extended his right. "I'm going to get out of here now. Before Ryan comes back. Congratulations."

I shook his hand. "Thanks."

"No problem."

He slid out the door connected to Pastor Dietz's office as silent as a ghost, and not five seconds later, the opposite door, the one that led into the sanctuary opened, and Ryan walked in. I could hear the murmur of the waiting crowd as he eased the door shut.

He glanced around the room, sniffing the air. "What's that flowery smell?"

I sniffed, too, and shrugged. "I don't smell anything."

"Smells like…" he sniffed the air again. "Lavender."

"It's probably from the flowers in the sanctuary or someone's perfume."

"I guess," he said, and slid his eyes to the envelope in my hand. "Where'd you get that?"

I glanced down at the envelope. I'd forgotten I was holding it. The flap was open, revealing the stack of crisp hundred-dollar bills. "From the EnviroTek guys. They all pitched in on a wedding gift."

He strummed his fingers over the top of the cash. "Looks like enough money to buy a car."

I scoffed. "It's only a couple of thousand dollars."

"I didn't know any of them were coming."

"They're not. They mailed it."

"To the church?"

"No," I chuckled lightly. "To my house. I put it in my jacket pocket this morning after I checked the mail before heading up here." I pointed at my jacket slung over a chair in the corner as though that would validate my story. "I forgot it was there until a second ago when I was checking the jacket pockets for my wallet." I crossed the room, put the envelope in my jacket pocket, and abruptly changed the subject. "Where'd you go anyway?"

A sneaky grin appeared on his face as he slipped a flask from his inner jacket pocket. "I figured we needed to have a pre-wedding toast. You know, to take the edge off." He passed me the flask. "Husbands first."

Take the edge off. Just like Luther had said.

I raised the flask. "To family." I chugged half the Vodka. It burned my throat and made my eyes water, adding to the comfort Luther had provided.

"To family," Ryan agreed, and downed the other half.

The wedding was a typical small wedding except the intro and exit music. Rather than classic organ music, Smashing Pumpkins' Today led Brianne down the aisle, and Tonight,

Tonight led us out. Smashing Pumpkins had been her favorite band since her teen years when she'd had a massive crush on Billy Corgan.

All my co-workers from Howe's came, Dan and his wife included. Brianne's mom, co-workers, and a group of her friends from high school came as well. Lucy, Jimmy, and Brenda brought Dad, but had to leave before the reception because he was having a bad day and kept cursing at random people who touched him. Pastor Dietz and some of the Lutheran congregation helped set up tables for the reception and treated us like members of their church family.

Sera was the maid of honor. She wore a gorgeous purple dress and had a matching purple flower in her hair that she later told me was Lilac. She'd picked it from Brenda's backyard. Her radiant smile never faltered. Not even when tears of joy leaked from her eyes at the end of the ceremony.

Ryan was the best man, and unlike me, was seemingly comfortable sporting a tuxedo. He puffed out his chest like a strutting peacock as he waltzed around the reception greeting people and flirting with some of Brianne's friends. His loud laughter was heard with regularity throughout the evening. No matter where you were, the bathroom, kitchen, out front having a smoke under the elm tree with the watchful blue jays overhead, when you heard the laugh, you knew who it was.

Brianne's dress wasn't the grand white mess I've seen women wear on TV. It was white, but simple and sleek and so perfectly form-fitting I found it hard to keep my eyes off her backside and chest. Although she wasn't one for dressing up (I could count on two hands how many times I'd seen her in a dress), and although any day of the week I'd prefer her braless and make-up free in sweat pants and a tank with her hair pulled back, she was stunningly beautiful. She smiled with her whole face when her eyes met mine for the first time. I hoped she could tell I wanted to be there, was proud to be there.

While dancing at the reception, I told her so to be sure she knew.

Fourteen

Is that Blood on Your Hand?

Nearly five months passed. My bank account grew. The blue jays stayed close. No new reports aired about missing Boulevard prostitutes. I tried to act as normal as possible. I made it a point to have drinks with the guys at Wizzards sometimes. Ryan moved out of his mom's apartment and got an efficiency apartment of his own. Howe's landed a contract to build a Latino-themed bar on the south end of Mercy. Sera developed more into a woman every day. Every minute it seemed. And I received less complaining from Brianne about being distant. We had a short honeymoon in South Padre Island where we lounged under umbrellas on the beach all day, drinking Marguritas and laughing, ate seafood in local restaurants as the sun dipped into the water at sunset, and spent gobs of time naked in bed.

Day-to-day life sailed by smooth enough that I had large gaps of time when I didn't think about Luther or notice the birds. Toward the end of the five months, I could almost go an entire day without thinking about Luther. And the times I did, I didn't have only dreadful, depressing thoughts. I allowed myself to hope that he'd been killed somehow, that the birds were on autopilot, carrying out an old order, and they'd all eventually disappear. Maybe it was over. But that hope ended after I had a few drinks at Wizzards with the guys one Thursday night.

I didn't notice the flyers on the trucks and cars in the parking lot until Ryan jerked one off his small Toyota's windshield. "Jesus-fucking-Christ. Goddamn son-of-a-Jew. Church of Christ says we all need to be saved…again," he said, followed by a burp and chuckle. He wadded up the flyer, tossed it on the ground, and pointed at me. A couple of the other guys who had parked close by stopped to listen. "Remember that fucking bird that night at your place?" he asked. "That one that attacked me?"

"I do," I said, "That was crazy. Never seen anything like it."

"What happened?" someone else asked.

"It fucking dive-bombed my face when I went to grab a flyer someone left on Seth's truck. But of course…" He squatted, cocked his arms at ninety-degree angles and swiped them through the air like he was Bruce Lee. He made a *waaaaaa* noise, stopped in an attack pose, then added, "It didn't know who it was messing with. I chopped the fucker right out of the air. Right, Seth?"

I thought of more than one witty comeback, but the reality of what had happened that night blanketed the humor behind them. I settled on a light "yeah," dropped my eyes to the pavement, and made my way toward my truck, fearful of what I'd find on the windshield. Behind me, Ryan resumed chopping at the night air, demanding the bird return for another battle.

The flyer on my windshield was the same yellow Church of Christ one Ryan had tossed on the ground. Relieved, I drove home with my hand swimming out the open window, surfing the waves of air like I had when I was a child.

At home, I parked behind Brianne's Fit, which was under the carport, then rolled the trash can to the dumpster in the alley behind the duplex to empty it. After taking a quick piss behind the dumpster, I was rolling the can back around the side of the duplex when a blue jay swooped down from the carport and landed on the lid. It had a note lodged in its beak. My heart jumped from idle to fifth gear as I slowly took the note. The bird waited while I read.

Hope your marriage is going well, friend. It's been a long while, but I think you know what to do.

I handed the note back to the bird and stood perfectly still staring down at the trash can as it flew away. I made my way back to the truck and glanced at the burlap sack. As I pulled away from the curb, I heard Brianne call my name from the front porch, but I didn't stop. I honked and threw my hand out the window and waved to let her know I was okay, then headed to the Latino-themed bar site.

I parked behind the rectangular building, next to the Bobcat and a front loader. The frame and sheetrock on the bar's main building was complete, and we had plans to pave the parking lot the following week.

The location was unlit and far enough away from high traffic areas that I could use the Bobcat to speed up the process. The closest building was two city blocks away— a warehouse with a giant, cheap *XXX VIDEO* sign haphazardly hung on the front. I dug in the center of what would six days later become the parking lot, retrieved the burlap sack, and was ten feet away from the hole when the person inside moved. And moaned.

I dropped the sack and jumped away from it as if it were explosive. "Please, God, don't let it move again."

I repeated the request three or four times before it jerked, and a loud, animalistic moan-groan seeped out of the sack and soured my ears. A bite of panic grabbed my chest. What was I supposed to do? Bury the person alive? Set them free? My eyes skidded to the hole. Two blue jays were hopping around the edge of it in geometric patterns as if dancing the cha-cha.

"It's just involuntary death spasms," I whispered, trying to convince myself. "That's all." I'd learned about death spasms from Dr. Biden on that HBO *Autopsy* show.

Extending my arm to maximum length, I inched toward the sack. When close enough, I grabbed a handful of burlap and took off running for the hole, dragging the sack behind me.

The birds moved aside, allowing me the room to slide the sack into the hole. When it landed in the bottom, a flurry of jerks and moans followed. I hurried to the Bobcat and started it up, but when I raised the first scoop of dirt to dump in the hole, I shut it off. I couldn't do it. What if the person was alive? I couldn't bury anyone alive. I couldn't be responsible for killing them.

I stepped off the Bobcat and knelt beside the hole. After taking a few measured breaths to steel myself, I loosened the knot that was keeping the sack closed and moved back.

Nothing happened. No head with horrified, dying eyes emerged. No desperate hand popped out, reaching for me.

Bug-eyed and anticipating the worst, I waited a moment before whispering, "Hello."

No movement. No response.

"Hello," I tried a little louder.

Still, nothing.

I nudged the mass in the sack with my foot. Nothing. I nudged again. Nothing. Maybe it *was* just death spasms, I thought.

I stood, took off my lucky Rangers hat, and was wiping the sweat off my face when my cell phone vibrated in my pocket, causing me to flinch and drop my hat into the hole. "Damn it," I mumbled as I checked my phone. It was a text from Brianne: *Where did you go? Worried.* I put the phone back in my pocket, then dropped down into the hole to retrieve my hat.

As I reached for the cap's bill, I heard a soft plea. "Help."

I froze with my arm extended.

"Help."

I stayed motionless for many long minutes, watching, listening, but I didn't hear anything else. Eventually, holding my breath, I grabbed the top of the burlap sack and eased it open to look inside, to make sure the person wasn't alive.

Short black hair clung to a woman's scalp like a beanie. Her large eyes were closed, dark-skinned cheeks and chin smeared with fresh blood.

"Hello," I whispered. "Are you alive?"

She didn't answer, but seconds later, her leg slightly twitched and I jumped back. Pressing my spine against the wall of the hole, I watched the sack for what felt like hours before reaching down and jerking it off the rest of her body.

Her knees were pulled up to her chest, hands clasped together, as though in prayer. Her nails were painted pink. She had on a purple tank top and cut-off jean-shorts. No bra. A fat trail of fresh blood stemming from a wound on her neck colored her chest. I put my hand on her shoulder. She was cold but not stiff. "Hey? Lady?"

She didn't move.

Holding my breath, I lowered my ear to her parted lips but didn't feel any air. I put my hand on her chest, my palm resting in her warm blood, but didn't feel any signs of breathing or heartbeats. I placed my fingers on her neck above the wound to check for a pulse but again felt nothing. She was dead. I was certain. But I was also certain I'd heard her whisper. Hadn't I?

My eyes cut to the two blue jays dancing around the hole, and an eerie sensation caused my stomach to tighten. Were they fucking with me? Could they do that? Or was I going crazy. Was my guilty conscience manipulating my imagination? Could I have imagined her movements and whispers? I wasn't sure. In that moment, I wasn't sure of anything other than the fact that I wanted to get the hell out of there.

As I leaned over the woman's body to grab my hat, her leg jerked. I tried to back up, but my feet tangled and I fell on top of her, chest to chest, face to face. I could smell her cheap perfume mixed with the coppery scent of her blood. Her perky breasts squashed into my chest, and she seemed to be smiling now, as if pleased I was mounting her.

In frantic, forceful movements, I used her face and body as leverage to push myself to my feet. Then, driven by panic and fear, I kicked her ten solid times in the face and abdomen. She never moved or moaned or tried to block or dodge the blows. She never asked for help, either. She just laid there and took it like a helpless dead person.

I regretted kicking her seconds after I finished. Even though she was dead, she didn't deserve to take the brunt of my frustration and fear and paranoia. She didn't deserve to be disrespected in that way. Not after she'd already lost her life… her family…been murdered by a monster and stuffed into a sack and discarded as trash.

After grabbing my hat and laying the bag over the woman's body, I jumped out of the hole, sprinted to the Bobcat, and quickly finished the job.

Foolishly figuring I'd just wash the woman's blood off my hands with the front yard hose, and that I'd take my shirt off before I went inside to talk with Brianne, I sped toward home. In hind-sight, I should've gone to a Toot 'n Totum or McDonald's bath-room to clean up instead. But at the time, my craving for the comfort of home, the sight of a comforting face, sound of a com-forting, real voice, overrode my better judgment.

Two blocks from the duplex, my cell phone vibrated. Assuming it was Brianne again, I didn't check it. I'd see her in a few seconds. I'd tell her I went to help one of the guys from work who was having car trouble and that I was sorry I hadn't told her where I was going. I wanted to help the guy and get home as quick as possible. To get into bed with her. Wink. Wink. But then I'd accidentally hit a dog and had to deal with that, too. That's why I hadn't answered her text.

After I parked behind Brianne's Fit, but before I killed the engine, a pair of headlights pulled in behind me. I glanced in the rearview mirror, and when I saw Ryan getting out of his truck, I quickly took off my bloody shirt and wadded it into a ball.

As I tossed it onto the floorboard, Ryan tapped on the window. He was smiling. I opened the door and stepped out.

"Did Brianne call you?" I asked.

"Yeah. She said you came home and took out the trash, but then left without talking to her. She was freaking out so I told her I'd see if I could find you."

I flashed a half-hearted smile. "Well, you found me."

He pointed at my chest. "Yeah. Shirtless. What the hell?"

I reflexively moved my right hand over my bare chest. What a mistake.

Ryan eye-balled my hand. "Is that blood on your hand?"

I glanced at my hand, opened and closed my fingers a few times as though I'd just learned the trick of finger movement. "Yeah," I admitted. "Dog blood," I lied.

"How did you get dog blood on you?"

I stared at my hand for a long moment. "One of my friends called right after I got home from Wizzards. He was at the Taco Villa on 45th street and wanted to know if I could come jump his car for him since I lived close by. On the way over there, a stupid mutt ran out in front of me, and I clipped it."

"Is it all right? Did it die?"

"No. He had a cut on its hind leg, but when I tried to see if he had tags, he ran off. He had a little hitch in his step but moved pretty well. I think he'll be fine." I thumbed at my shirt on the floorboard. "Got a little blood on my shirt, too. That's why I took it off."

He nodded, but his brow furrowed. "Did you go ahead and go help...who was it that called you?"

The simple question tripped me up. I'd prepared the fib for Brianne, not Ryan. I could get away with stretching the truth about the guys from work with her. She knew some of them but not all. She also understood that turnaround was high, the grunt workers coming and going quicker than nails from a nail-gun. And based on her opinion of Dan, and Howe's in general, I don't think she listened much when I went off about work anyway.

Ryan, on the other hand, knew everyone I worked with. Well. Better than I did in most cases. He may not have been blessed with math or English smarts, but he could look someone in the eye and shake their hand once (even when sloppy drunk or high as a kite) and recall their name ten years later if he came across them. A politician's trait if there ever was one.

"Uh...it was...this guy named Darren. He doesn't work with us anymore."

"I don't remember any Darren."

I dropped my eyes to my bloody hand for a moment, twisted it side to side, looked up. "Yeah. He worked there before you came on board I think."

He nodded, but I could tell by the look in his eyes that he didn't buy it. That he wanted to know more. Ask more questions. He was a people person by nature and could smell a bullshit story mile away. For both our sakes, I didn't want to give him the opportunity to press the issue.

"Well, I better get inside," I said. "I need to go apologize to Brianne. You know her. She's probably blown a gasket by now." I patted his shoulder. "Be safe. I'll see you at work in the morning." I hurried to the porch and glanced back over my shoulder.

Ryan was looming around the front of The Chevy, examining the fender. He ran his hand over the bumper. "Doesn't look like it did any damage," he said, and smiled. "But it would be hard to tell if this piece of shit clipped a meteor."

I held up a bloody, acknowledging hand, and then quickly went inside.

Fifteen

New Home, Same Problems

Neither Brianne nor I had ever owned a house, and she had only lived in cheap rental properties. Having a place of our own meant a great deal to me, but even a greater deal to her.

She never said so, but I think she saw owning a house as proof that she'd risen above her troubled upbringing. That she'd bested her past, her mom, her drunkard dad who she hadn't spoken to since she was ten. Some people need a college education to feel that. Others need the notoriety associated with becoming a doctor or lawyer. Or landing a role in a blockbuster movie. Others need a higher calling from God or Allah or Jehovah, helping the poor or saving souls from the fires of Hell. Brianne needed a house. A permanent home.

In August, a few months after I'd kicked and buried the woman at the Latino bar site, one week before Sera started her freshman year at Mercy High, and two years after I'd met Luther, we closed on a two-story brick home in Ridgecrest. It was the last house on a dead-end street on the northwestern edge of Mercy. Eighty-year-old cottonwoods surrounded the house. Beyond the backyard, open plains rolled as far as the eye could see.

The house was built in the 1930s but had been renovated in the late '90s. "Classic charm with modern comforts" was how our realtor described it. It had four spacious bedrooms, a large kitchen, a living room, and a den. Our furniture didn't fill half the house, our plates and cups and pots and pans not even a third of the storage space in the kitchen. We spent every weekend for a month shopping for new tables, sofas, and other various decorative pieces. Brianne picked out a new bedroom set for us. All but our queen-size bed. We'd bought it at a garage sale when we moved in to the duplex together, and she thought it would be bad luck to switch it out.

We gave Sera her pick of the three bedrooms upstairs. She picked the one with the most windows—four. One window looked out over the driveway and detached garage, the other three, the backyard. We also let her pick out her own bedroom furniture, which tickled her to no end. We spent two days hopping from antique shop to antique shop because she wanted to "go vintage." She bought an oak, hand-carved queen-size headboard, a '40s-style dresser with a large mirror, a metal vanity, and a small desk that came from a school that was abandoned in the '50s.

The backyard was as large as the entire lot our old duplex sat on and had a wrap-around porch like the one on that farmhouse in *Field of Dreams*. We bought a wooden swing for the porch that Ryan helped me assemble, and Brianne hung a couple of asparagus ferns in macramé holders on either side of it.

My dad and Brenda helped us unload the U-Haul the day we moved in, and we offered Dad the apartment above the detached garage (It had its own stove and fridge, toilet and tub.), but he refused, of course, saying he'd rather die in his own home thank you very much.

Ryan came by the house nearly every day in the beginning. He helped us paint the bedrooms, replace a few splintered doors and broken outlets, and re-tile one of the showers. Like Dad, we offered him the apartment, free of rent, and like Dad, he refused, saying he liked finally having a place of his own, even if it was just a small efficiency. He said he was saving for a house of his own, too. I think it's safe to say he had the same craving for a permanent home as Brianne.

Personally, I liked everything about the new house—the spacious yard, the architecture, the layout, the size, mostly, the sparkle it brought to Brianne's and Sera's eyes—but I never felt as comfortable there as I hoped I would. No matter how far back in mind I tried to push the truth, no matter how hard I reminded myself that owning a house was a dream come true for Brianne, knowing the true cost of the house, dwelling on it, seeing it right in front of me every morning I woke up, made that next to impossible.

Because her bedroom windows faced the backyard, it didn't take Sera long to notice that two blue jays had built nests in the largest cottonwood and that they regularly hung out in the shade on the back porch ledge.

When I came home from work one evening, I found her standing on a stepladder, hanging two bird feeders under the porch eaves. Her face, hands, and T-shirt were splattered with different colors of paint. There were even a few drops stuck in her curls.

"What are you doing?" I asked.

She giggled. "What's it look like, silly?"

The way she enunciated the word silly brought a silly smile to my face. Esperanza's preference for words and Latino accent had seemingly reached across space and time and smacked Sera right in the mouth. Looking up to keep from staring at her in that awkward way parents do their kids sometimes, I examined the feeder closest to me. They were tall, thin wood feeders with a pointed roof. "Where'd you get these?"

"Brianne took me to Hobby Lobby after school today. I painted them myself."

The sides of the one I was looking at were painted purple, the roof grey. It had the name PAUL painted above the food-hole, large blue diamonds on either side. "Why Paul?" I asked.

"You always said one of Mom's favorite bands was The Beatles, right?"

I nodded. "Yeah."

"And I think the two blue jays that built their nests in that tree right after we moved in are the same two we saw at the graveyard that day. I think Mom sent them here to protect us. So I named one of them Paul and the other..." She proudly marched over and showed me the feeder she was about to hang. It was solid blue with white smudges that I assumed were clouds. JOHN was painted above the feed-hole, a pair of wire rim glasses below the letters. "I named John. I think that's what she would've done, don't you?"

I kissed the top of her head and agreed, wishing her take on the situation were the truth. I wanted it to be the truth so strongly that a ball of emotion swelled in my throat, making it hard for me to swallow or talk.

Those feeders were emptied daily once word spread among the neighborhood birds that free seeds were available at the Fowler residence. But I never once saw one of the two blue jays eat from them.

Sixteen

Leave Me Alone!

A blue jay landed in front of the back porch swing when I was home alone drinking beer one fall Friday night. Brianne was working a closing shift at the Golden Corral, and Sera was staying the night at a friend's house. When I saw the note pinched in its sharp beak my immediate reaction was to kick at it. "Leave me alone," I hollered. On top of all the lying and pretending and burials and nightmares, I'd had a rough week at work. Dan was riding my ass about finishing two rebuilds we were working on for a rental property company.

Unfazed, the blue jay hopped onto the armrest, dropped the note on my leg, fluttered back down onto the porch.

Congratulations on the new house. I need to come see it sometime.

You know what to do.

I wadded up the note and tossed it at the blue jay. It dodged left, plucked it off the ground, and flew away. I downed the last of my beer and left.

I killed my headlights as I turned down the alley that ran behind the rental properties. They were on Galahad Street, the outermost street in a large middle-class neighborhood. A brick storage unit lined the side of the alley opposite the houses, an open lot and abandoned grocery store behind that, providing a sense of security. I parked behind house 216, which was almost complete. That morning the privacy fence had gone up and sod had been laid in the front and back yards. The paint would be done Monday.

On the drive over, I'd decided to dig the hole in the corner next to the fence that separated the two backyards. Since the sod was freshly laid, I'd peel up a few squares, do the deed, and lay them back down.

After grabbing a shovel from the Chevy (I couldn't risk the Bobcat. Lit residential houses lined the other side of Galahad.), I was on my way back to the yard when a pair of headlights pulled into the alley and stopped behind my truck. I crouched in front of my hood, hoping whoever it was would realize the way was blocked and back out. But the lights went out. I stayed still and silent, my pulse racing. A few seconds later, when the engine cut off, I knew it was Ryan. A belt on his little Toyota made a sharp squeal when he shut it down. A dying cat squeal.

A door opened and closed. "Seth? Where are you?"

I rose as his footfalls approached. "Hey," I said. "What are you doing out here?"

"I was about to ask you the same thing," he answered. He had a beer in each hand and offered me one. I took it. "Why didn't you come to Willis's party?"

Willis was one of the workers. A roofer. He'd been on the team two years. He'd invited everyone to a birthday barbecue party at his house. I'd said I'd go, but when I learned Brianne and Sera wouldn't be home and I'd have the house to myself, I decided to stay home. "You know how it is." I chugged a third of my beer. "When I got home Sera needed a ride to her friend's house, and then I had to stop by the store to pick up a few things for Brianne, and by the time I got back home and remembered, it was too late."

He swiped his hand through the air like a magician's assistant displaying a miraculously empty box. "And so you choose to come out here instead?" He lowered his hand, took a sip. "Didn't you get your fill of work shit today at *work*?"

"Guess not." I took a drink. "How come you're here?"

"When I didn't find you at your house or Wizzards, I figured you'd be out here. Those are the only three places you go these days. Home, Wizzards, and work." He tilted his bottle at the shovel. "What are you going to do with that?"

My eyes fell to the shovel, the bed of my truck. A bubble of frustration expanding in my chest. I wanted to get the sack in the ground and get back home. I wanted to be alone. I didn't want to be answering questions. Making up lies. Chit-chatting with Ryan while a corpse was in the back of my truck. Unable to come up with a specific answer, I said, "I just wanted to check on some stuff."

"What stuff?"

My grip tightened on both the shovel and beer bottle. "Just stuff, all right? You wouldn't understand."

He laughed, causing beer to spew from his mouth onto my pant leg and shoe. "I understand Dan's influence on you is strong as stink on shit."

The bubble inside my chest burst. "You don't get it. You'll never get it. You think everything's a fucking joke." I threw my beer bottle against the wall of the storage building, below a blue jay perched on the flat roof, watching, listening. Beer starred the wall and shards of glass flew into the alley.

"Chill out, man," Ryan said, raising his hands in the air in surrender. He set his bottle on the hood of my truck, took a step toward me.

I lifted the shovel off the ground. "You need to get out of here."

"You don't have to be an asshole."

I pointed toward his truck. "Leave," I ordered.

He spun and hurled his beer bottle at the wall. It hit exactly where mine had. "You've changed, man. I don't know if it's Dan, or the job, or Randy, or your dad's health, or the new money, but you've changed."

"Everybody changes," I said.

"Yeah." He thrust an accusatory finger at me. "But you've changed for the worse. Brianne was right."

"About what?"

"About questioning your actions before the wedding." He lowered his hand but kept his equally accusatory eyes locked on mine. "And I know that since then you've been coming out with the guys again, and Bri says you're more like your old self at home, but it's all an act. Something is still off inside you, and it's plain to see."

He was right. I felt different. I thought different. I was different. But there was nothing I could do about it. Besides, I was different for him. For Brianne. Sera. My dad.

He put his hands on his scrawny hips, tilted his head back, aiming his eyes at the stars, and breathed for a moment. When he leveled his eyes with mine, he said, "You know I love you like a brother. And I'm always here to talk if you want. But I won't put up with you being a dick to me."

"I don't want..." I started but trailed off. "What I want right now is for you to leave me alone."

He shook his head, a disbelieving smirk on his face.

"Leave me alone!" I yelled louder than I'd intended.

"Fine," he said, forcing the word out with anger. "Just what I'd expect you to say." He headed for his truck but stopped and turned around after he passed my driver's door. He eyed the bed for moment, sloshed his hand around inside close to the burlap sack, shaking his head.

"Don't touch my shit," I said.

He snapped his head at me, snatched the burlap sack, and hoisted it a foot into the air. My eyes bulged, heart hitched, and I bit my lip to keep from screaming at him to drop the damn corpse. After glancing at the watchful bird, I growled and slammed the shovel down onto my truck, mashing a dent the size of a football into the hood.

"What the fuck's wrong with you?" Ryan yelled. He rustled the sack still in his hand. "All this shit is just that...shit." He dropped the sack and pointed toward the newly erected fence. "And all that is just work. It's not what really matters." He pointed at me, then moved his finger to his own chest. "Me and you. We're family. That's what matters. You used to know that. What the hell happened, man?"

With the taste of warm blood on my tongue from biting my lip, I stared. Realizing I wasn't going to answer the question, he jumped into his truck, slammed the door, and peeled out of the alley, leaving me alone with my frustration. When he was out of sight, I slammed the shovel into my hood again. And again.

Ryan *was* like a brother to me. One of the closest friends I'd ever had. I truly loved him. But like Brianne, by no fault of his own, there was no way he could understand my intentions or motivations. I'd done what I had to do to get him away from a toxic situation. Treated him the way he had to be treated given the gravity of the situation. Because family *was* what mattered to me. He mattered to me.

Afraid he might return, or that someone had heard us arguing, or the shovel slam into my hood, or his truck speeding away, I tossed the shovel in the bed of my truck and left.

Gripping the wheel tight enough to whiten my knuckles, I drove to Plemons again. But this time after crossing the bridge, I went five miles further down the riverbed. I passed three vehicles head-on, two oil field trucks and one SUV that appeared to be stuffed with teens. I also saw four sets of headlights in my rearview mirror. A few before the burial, a few after. But I didn't see any lights or pass any cars after I turned off the main road and onto an old oil pump road crowded with crumbling mesquite and tall buffalo grass. Cursing Ryan for showing up at the rental property with each scoop and toss, I buried the body under the watchful eye of a blue jay.

Many months later I learned one of the sets of headlights I'd seen in my rearview was Ryan's. The dumbass had followed me.

Brianne and two of her friends from the Golden Corral had drinks at Whiskey River after work, and she didn't get home until 2AM that night. I pretended to be asleep when she whispered my name and kissed my head, and pretended again when she returned from showering, eased under the covers, and fell asleep. After dozing for an hour or two, I snuck out of bed just before sunrise, grabbed a beer from the fridge, and went to the back porch.

Ten seconds after my butt hit the swing, Luther called out my name.

I snapped my head and saw him standing at the end of the porch, fifteen feet away, leaning against the house next to the kitchen window with his hands in his pant pockets. He wore a green Guayabera, black slacks.

"How are you doing, my friend?" he asked. Two blue jays swooped down from the elm tree and landed at his feet, but he kept his eyes on me. "A little early for a drink, don't you think?"

I moved my attention to the yard. "To what do I owe the pleasure?"

He snickered. "What got your panties in a wad?"

I finished my beer and tossed the can into the yard. "I'm just tired. Got a lot on my mind."

"Ryan?"

"Yes. Ryan. Work. The..." My eyes met his. I didn't want to say "bodies" out loud. It somehow made it more real. "You know."

He pinched his lips together and nodded as though sympathetic. As though he were a concerned friend and my burden had nothing to do with him. "If you want I could help ease some of your worry," he said.

"I don't want you touching me right now."

"I wasn't talking about that." He moved away from the house, took a couple of steps forward, stopped, crossed his arms over his chest. "I was talking about eliminating the most pressing item off your worry list for you."

I knew exactly what he meant. An image of Ryan's vacant, lifeless close-set eyes staring at me from inside a burlap sack popped into my mind. "No. No way," I responded with vigor.

"He's almost caught you twice now. Once with the blood on your hand. And this time he actually picked up the sack. You got pretty damn lucky. If he gets any closer, I won't have a choice. He'll have to be eliminated. No one can find out, remember?"

"Of course I fucking remember," I snapped back. Then I took in a deep breath, released it. "I won't let him find out." Leaning forward, I propped my elbows on my knees and lay my head in my hands. I sat like that for a long minute, then admitted, "I don't' know if I can do this anymore."

"You don't have a choice," Luther said in a matter-of-fact, all-is-well tone. "You know that."

"Maybe if you just give me a break for a while. Stop paying me. Don't make me do any jobs. But you can let the birds keep watching me to make sure I don't say anything to anyone about you. Maybe if I had some time away from it I could...I don't know." I ground my palms into my eyes.

"That's not part of the deal you agreed to. Besides, it's not like I ask you to do it every day. Sometimes I don't call on you for months. And for what you're paid, I'd say that's a damn good deal."

"Why don't you just do it yourself?" I twisted my face toward him. "It would be so easy for you." I don't know why I asked. I knew he wouldn't shoot me a straight answer, give me what I believed to be the truth. He would never tell me he didn't want to get his hands dirty. That he wanted a patsy, a scapegoat, someone to take the fall if the bodies were found. And on a deeper level, he would never tell me he simply liked having someone to control. That he reveled in the power, the sense of superiority, the God-like status the control over me gave him. And on even a deeper level, he would never tell me that perhaps part of the reason he did it was because he was lonely, didn't want to live an isolated existence. Somewhere deep inside, he longed for a friend. Another brother.

He smirked. "You're right. It would be easy. But if I did it myself, you wouldn't have this." He tapped on the side of the house. "And Brianne wouldn't be your wife. Or have a Fit. And Ryan would still be in debt. And your dad wouldn't have proper care. And on and on. Just like I told you the night we met." He tapped his chest. "I like giving guys like you, guys who've gotten the shaft for a majority of their life, a chance to prosper."

"Then why not just help. Why the catch?" Again, I don't know why I asked. Did he really want to help me? Maybe a little. But only because keeping me happy lowered his risk of getting caught.

"I'm not a charity," he answered. "I give people that deserve a chance at a better life that chance. Giving away achievements as easy as handshakes just leads to laziness and a lack of appreciation."

"It's not a chance if you force it on them."

"In my line of business, choices create obstacles and lead to problems. That's just the way it is."

I sat up straight and snickered. "Line of business. Killing

people isn't a line of business."

"It's a necessity," he replied.

"How can it be a necessity?"

His eyes narrowed to two fierce flashing points, and he scrutinized me for a long while. "You're a smart man. I'm sure you have guesses as to how."

Tired and emotionally frustrated, I let the question that had been circling around in my head for more than a year slip out. "Are you a vampire or alien or something?"

"What is this? 1400?" He took another step toward me. The blue jays hopped along beside him. The hairs on the back of my neck stood in fearful anticipation. "I'm a unique individual with special interests and needs. Nothing more. Nothing less." He licked his lips. "What I have to do to survive is no more my fault than it is your dad's that he's losing his mind."

Although scared, I pressed him. "Why don't you just get whatever you need from animals like that guy in *Interview with a Vampire*?"

He shook his head slow and steady, as if the question were the stupidest question in the history of questions. "You fools do enough of that yourself. But you know what doesn't get done? No one weeds out the human population. The drug dealers, prostitutes, murderers, molesters, rapists. They all get chance after chance after chance no matter how many people they hurt. No matter how many diseases they spread. No matter how many children they abandon. Imagine how much better society would be without them."

He jerked his head toward the kitchen window and stepped away from the glass when a light inside flicked on. Water ran from the faucet for a moment, then the light went off. He pointed at me. "You make sure Ryan doesn't get any closer or else I will."

I nodded.

"And get your head on straight. Stop fucking thinking so much. You have a great life. If you don't stop worrying, you're not going to enjoy it. And then what would all this be for?" He shoved his hands in his pants pockets. "I'll be in touch," he said, and walked around the side of the house and out of sight.

Seconds later, Brianne came outside in her pink robe, a

mug of warm tea in her hand, and sat down next to me on the swing. She asked if I was having trouble sleeping and I said yes. We listened to the birds sing their morning songs as the sun appeared and climbed the horizon. When she went inside, I was glad to be alone.

Seventeen

Brianne's Blind-Side

The first couple of years after Brianne, Sera, and I had moved into the duplex, we'd spent many Saturday and Sunday afternoons treasure hunting at antique shops downtown. It was Brianne's idea. She'd wanted us to shop together, to have objects around the house that would connect us as a group. As a family.

On those days, we would search our nightstand drawers, empty the Chevy's ashtray, dig under the cushions on the sofa and recliner, clean out the pocket-bowl in the laundry room, and Sera would dump her piggy bank, looking for as much change as possible. Then we'd head down to 10th Street—a section of old Route 66 that had been transformed into an eight-block thrift/antique shop extravaganza—to see what treasure we could buy with the change we'd found.

The treasures never had any monetary value. We never spent more than six or seven dollars on any given day, and we never found that twenty-five cent painting that turned out to be a million-dollar Monet. But each item we found was a treasure to us.

The cloudy snow globe, ugly over-sized Cosby sweater, stuffed sock-puppet (Sera named him Stu and keeps on her bed to this day.), and odd trinkets like rusty key chains and bizarre scarves and ties that most people wouldn't be caught dead in, became our own little time capsules. They littered our duplex, each holding a secret, a day's journey and choice that only one of us three could explain. Sometimes one of us would pick an item up, show the others, and we'd all smile or laugh. It was like that.

But over time, for reasons I'm unsure of, the shopping trips became farther and farther apart and eventually faded into the past. Eight years into the past. Sometimes late at night when drunk on alcohol or sex, we reminisced about the shopping days, saying we should do it again someday, but we never had. Then one Saturday morning eight months ago, I woke to find Brianne scrounging for change under the couch cushions in the living room.

"Are you doing what I think you're doing?" I asked.

The corners of her mouth curved up in a smile that spread to her eyes. A similar smile formed on my face, and without asking why she had the sudden desire to revisit the past, I began searching as well. Thirty minutes later Sera was up and dressed and happily involved in the search. We left the house around 10AM with $9.43 in our pocket.

After visiting two stores without any item calling out to us, Brianne, who seemed distracted and had been holding my hand tighter and longer than usual, stopped on the corner of 10th and Georgia, grabbed the back of my shirt when I kept moving, and spun me around. Sera stopped behind us.

Brianne's eyes flicked from Sera's to mine. "I need to tell you guys something," she said, obviously nervous. Her hand was balmy.

"What?" I asked.

She blinked slowly, then said, "I'm pregnant."

"Are you sure?" I asked as Sera squealed like a mouse and hugged Brianne. As far as I knew, she was on birth control. She had been since she was sixteen.

"I took a home test four days ago and went to Dr. Stevens to confirm it yesterday."

I pulled her against my chest and wrapped my arms around her. "That's great," I said, her behavior over the last month suddenly making sense. Her new health food kick. Her picking up extra shifts at work to "save for the future." Her latest and best attempt to stop smoking. The desire to revisit treasure shopping.

She pulled away and wiped the moisture from her eyes before it could escape.

"This baby is destined for greatness," I said, half-serious and half-joking. "I mean... how many babies are born when the woman's on birth control?"

She searched my eyes for a moment, then said, "I stopped taking the pill almost six months ago." When I didn't immediately respond, she added, "I was going to tell you but you were stressed about work, and I didn't want to add..." She looked down, fidgeted with her nails, looked up. "You know I'm approaching the dreaded thirty-five. At my last checkup Dr. Stevens said that after thirty-five the chance for miscarriage, or having a child with Down's syndrome or autism or any other horrifying problem, drastically increased. He said if I ever wanted a child, now was the best—"

I placed my finger on her lips. "It's all right," I said, and she laid her head on my chest and exhaled deeply. "Is that why you wanted to come shopping again? To buy something new as a family like we used to?"

She nodded.

"When do we find out if it's a boy or a girl...or twins?" Sera asked with the eagerness of a child picking out their first puppy. "And when do we find out when the due date is?"

"Not for a while," Brianne said. "You can go to the doctor with me next time and ask him if you want."

Sera wrapped her arms partially around Brianne, partially me. Her curls tickled my mouth, and I turned my head to the side. "I'm going to be a big sister," she said, happily stomping her sandals on the sidewalk a couple of times.

As I stood there with my two girls in my arms, I glanced up and saw a slew of missing persons fliers taped on a glass window behind them. Amber Powell's giant eyes jumped out at me. She would have been twenty-one the following month based on her birthdate on the flier. Of course I had the unfortunate knowledge that she would never celebrate that birthday. She would remain twenty forever.

To the right of Amber's picture was Staci Umbarger's water-damaged pink flier. Twenty-eight, single, loved to ballet dance, the flier said. I didn't recognize her face, didn't know if I'd carried her to her final resting place, but she'd been one of the girls named on the news report I'd seen at my dad's house.

I let my eyes slide over the remaining seven or eight fliers but not long enough to read the names. I closed my eyes tight and tried to think about the baby. What he or she may look like, be like. I tried to think about Brianne holding the baby, Sera playing with it. I tried to think about the positive, I did. But I couldn't get the sight of Amber Powell's eyes out of my head.

"Are you all right?" Brianne asked after we'd hugged for a long while.

Smiling thinly, I opened my eyes. "Fine. A little shocked. But fine."

She pressed her lips to mine. In that moment, with her warm lips on mine, our bean-size baby snuggled between us, Sera looking on with a delighted expression on her face, and the large, accusatory eyes of Amber Powell boring into my heart, reminding me that she was someone's baby, that they all were, a breaker tripped inside my head and I knew I had to find a way to end my relationship with Luther. I had to take back control over my life.

I couldn't keep burying his victims and prolonging their family's pain. I couldn't keep lying to my family. I couldn't allow the guilt and fear to continue eating away at me, chewing up any happiness I happened on. I had a baby on the way. A long life ahead of me. I had to find a way out. I just had to. But it had to be a way that wouldn't endanger my family. And although the idea scared the shit out of me, I knew there was only one way to absolutely secure my family's safety. I would have to kill Luther...if he could die. There was no other option. He'd reminded more than once that I could never just quit and go on my merry way. Our agreement was for life.

As we continued shopping, Sera demanded we find something for the baby. In the two-story labyrinth of a building called Alley Cats, she found a light blue, hand-knitted baby beanie with a sunflower on it. She said it would work for a girl or a boy and Brianne agreed. It cost $4.95. She also located a scratched-up plastic rattle from the late 50's or early 60's. It had a guitar on it and cost $6.95, which would put us over our limit. So she marched the rattle up to the register and told the owner, Gwendolyn, an elderly woman with red hair and thick glasses who'd sold us the cloudy snow globe eight years earlier, about our spending limit and the baby (which Brianne didn't seem to like much), and the woman said she could have the rattle for three bucks, keeping us under our limit.

Eighteen

Anonymous Tip

When we arrived home that afternoon with the rattle and beanie and I saw the blue jays sitting in the front yard, staring at me, I felt more vulnerable than I had since the first time Luther had laid his hand on me in my truck and forced immeasurable fear into me. I was terrified that somehow he would know my unspoken decision, be aware of my secret intentions. Or that the blue jays would somehow know, or somehow find out, and would relay the message to him. I had no idea how deep Luther's mental or psychological reach went. But I knew how sincere his threats were.

Based on our conversations, I didn't think he could read minds. But hearts? Desires? Intentions? I didn't know. There were a lot of things I didn't know about him, but I had no doubts that he'd only shown me the tip of his abilities.

With an uneasy, desperate feeling prodding me, compelling me, I headed to my dad's house after dinner to get my guns. I didn't know if Luther could die by a bullet, or at all for that matter, but putting my family's life at risk for an unknown wasn't an option. I had to have something to try and protect us in case he found out and paid us a visit.

As a kid, I'd gone deer and turkey hunting with my dad. He berated me most of the time, calling me loud and stupid and clumsy, but my mom made him take me a couple of times each fall, and I have some good memories. In my teens, I stopped going with Dad and would go alone, or with my friend Tommy. Once I started working full time after high school, I pretty much stopped hunting. I can count on one hand how many times I've gone in the past fifteen years, although me and Ryan would occasionally take a twelve pack down to the river and shoot at bottles and cans. I took Esperanza once, too. She was a damn good shot. She said her dad had taught her how to shoot. They regularly cleared the area behind their house in Mexico of prairie dogs.

My arsenal wasn't large or spectacular. I had a .22 rifle my mom and dad had gotten me for Christmas when I was sixteen, and I had a 9MM handgun I'd bought from of one my co-workers at Howe's who'd fallen on hard times and needed cash. The guns were at my dad's because Brianne wouldn't allow guns in her house, and I didn't bother fighting her when we moved in together and she insisted I keep them somewhere else. When she was eleven, one of her friends in the apartment complex they lived in found her daddy's gun and accidentally shot herself in the face. Brianne found the girl, blood and brains leaking from her head, coloring her blonde hair crimson. The one time she told me the story was one of the few times I ever saw her cry.

I planned on sneaking the guns into our house and hiding them well, and after I'd taken care of Luther, I'd sneak them back to Dad's place. If I was careful (and lucky), she would never know they'd been there.

When I arrived at Dad's house, a couple of blue jays flew over my head and landed in the dead elm in the front yard. I opened the front door and found Brenda and Dad sitting on the couch flipping through photo albums.

"Hey," I said. "What's going on?" Brenda looked up at me. Dad appeared exhausted. His eyes were bloodshot, his cheeks dry and ruddy, like they'd been scrubbed with sandpaper.

Brenda tried to give me her classic motherly smile, but something was missing from it. "We're just looking at old pictures," she said. The way she said it, the way her eyes searched mine, I knew there was more she wanted to tell me, but not in front of Dad.

"Can you come outside for a second, Brenda?" I asked. "I wanted to ask you something about that bush on the side of your house."

"Sure." She patted Dad's thigh. "Be right back."

Dad didn't look up as we stepped outside onto the porch and closed the door behind us.

"What's wrong?" I asked.

"Well, I came to check on him like I do every Saturday and Sunday, you know, on Lucy's days off, and I found him sitting there cursing and crying looking at those albums."

"Why's he crying?"

"He's angry because he can't remember some of the people and places in the pictures. And he was yelling at me because I didn't know some of them either."

"How long have you been here?"

"Since about one, I guess."

I closed my eyes, tipped my head back, and shook my head. "I'm sorry. I need to hire someone to watch him on the weekends so you don't have to come over here and—"

"I've told you," She cut in, touching my forearm lightly, as though it would shatter if she put too much force on it. "I come because I want to, not because I have to. He's family to me, too. Besides, he's just having a bad day. Not every day is like this."

"I know, but as he gets worse, I'll have to—"

She cut me off again, using the same advice that my mom would've given had she been there. "We'll deal with that when it happens. Not now."

"You're right," I admitted, nodding. "Thanks for coming by. I'll stay with him until he falls asleep. Maybe I'll even stay the night."

"Okay, Honey. Try and get him to eat something, too. He refused to eat dinner for me."

I nodded again.

"And holler if you need anything. You know where I am."

I watched Brenda make her way to her house, waved when she reached the front door, then went inside and sat with Dad.

We flipped through two or three albums. Unprovoked, I named the people in each picture and said what I knew about them. When they were taken, where, etc. Dad stared at the pictures with a serious expression on his face, as if studying for an important exam. He flipped the pages and nodded at my explanations, although only occasionally commented. He never asked where Brenda went or why I was there.

We spent a good hour looking. Some of my favorite pictures were of me and mom. The Polaroid pictures taken while Dad was at work, while Mom and I were deep in the heart of Lurth, playing, adventuring, escaping. Of course I didn't tell Dad the truth behind those pictures, or what the letter labels Mom had written on the thick white strips on the bottom meant. I told him, "Here's me and Mom jacking around with the camera when I was four or five again." He didn't seem too interested and only asked once what the letters were for.

One photo had LLFT written below it in Mom's bubbly letters. I told him I had no idea what they meant. "Mom must have done it," I said. But I knew. The picture showed me wearing a pair of ears we'd made with construction paper and one of Mom's headbands. I had my arm draped over my stuffed teddy bear that also had pointy paper ears, a paper horn, and two paper tails. LLFT stood for Lenny Lummox's Field Trip. Mom and I took my special pet, Lenny, on a field trip in Lummorville that afternoon. We took him to the rainbow forest (the bathroom with colorful strips of construction paper taped to the mirror and hanging from the ceiling), and to Piddler's Pond (the bath tub filled with water tainted red with food coloring; sponges we'd cut into weird shapes floating around) where time slowed to a crawl, allowing Lenny to bask in the sun beside the pond for as long as he wished and listen to the song of the Lurdlings (small bird-like creatures we'd made from boiled eggs and construction paper sitting on the edge of the tub and the windowsill).

After an hour of looking, I asked Dad if he wanted something to eat and he nodded. I heated him up two bean and cheese burritos, took them into the living room, and popped in one of his favorite Clint Eastwood movies, *Pale Rider.* As he ate and watched, I snuck the albums back up into the attic, then retrieved my two guns from the locked gun case in the garage. I wrapped the rifle in an old striped quilt Mom had started on but never finished. The blue jays would be waiting outside when I left, and I didn't want them seeing the guns. The less they knew, the less they could tell Luther, the better. Sure, simply carrying a gun didn't necessarily mean I was going to use it on Luther, or that it was related to my relationship with him whatsoever, but my paranoid mind *knew* they would assume that.

I asked Dad if he needed anything else or if he wanted me to stay the night with him. He gave me a quick, *are-you-fucking-kidding-me* eye-shot, and then flicked his eyes back to the TV screen. Holding the rifle wrapped in the quilt parallel to my leg, I told him I loved him and headed out the front door. He either didn't notice the quilt, or the jingle of bullets in my pocket, or the bulge in the back of my pants where the 9MM was stuffed in my waistband, or he didn't care.

I had shoved the 9MM under the seat of The Chevy and was about to lay the quilt in the bed when I heard a car pull up behind me. I glanced over my shoulder and saw that it was Detective Morrell. I hurriedly lay the quilted-rifle down and walked to greet him by the tailgate. Smiling, I extended my hand, and he shook it.

"How are you, Seth?" he asked.

I shoved my hands in my pockets and curled my fingers around the bullets. "Good."

"How's your dad?" he asked. During our talks after Randy vanished, I'd told him about Dad's condition.

"He had a bad afternoon, but he seems to be doing better now."

Morrell nodded, then cut his droopy eyes at the bed of the truck. "What's in the quilt?"

I glanced at it, back at him. "Oh, that's my .22. Brianne won't let me keep guns at the house, and I wanted to go target shooting down at the river tomorrow so..."

He nodded again, but didn't say anything. My heart was hammering, hands growing sweaty in my pockets.

"What brings you over here?" I asked.

"Well, I needed to ask you a few questions about Randy."

I widened my eyes, trying for a hopeful look. Morrell's blank expression didn't change much, but it changed enough for me to know that his bullshit detector was on high alert. "Did you find out something new?" I asked.

He shook his head. "Nope. But tips keep trickling in. The most recent involved you."

"Okay," I said, carrying out the *aaayyyy* as if his statement baffled me.

He pulled a notepad out of his breast pocket, flipped to a page filled with words, and slid his eyes back and forth a few times as though he needed the notes to remind him what he came to ask me. "We had a caller tell us they think you may know more about Randy's disappearance then you've let on."

"*What?* Who?"

"Anonymous."

"I don't... I've told you everything I know." It was hard to tell whether he believed me or not. "Did they tell you anything specific I *should* know?"

He scratched his head. "Did you and Randy ever go down to the Boulevard together to look for dates?"

"*Dates?*"

"Yeah. You know, pick up a woman for an hour or two of fun?"

"You mean hookers?"

"Did you guys like to pick up hookers?"

"No," I said emphatically.

"Do you know if Randy liked to pick up hookers?"

I knew he had. He'd bragged about it several times. "I think so. Sometimes. But I was never with him when he did. Why?"

Morrell lazily scratched his ear. "Well, we have reason to believe he may be connected to some of the missing Boulevard girls. Have you heard about that? The missing girls?"

I nodded. "Sure. I saw it on the news a while back. Why do you think he's connected to that?"

"Well, talk on the Boulevard is that he favored a few of the missing girls, if you know what I mean. Some people say he didn't treat women that well, either. Brianne even said this much the first time we talked to you guys. Can you tell me everything you know about his relationship troubles?"

"I told you everything I know right after he went missing. I don't know anything else."

"Do you think Brianne knows anything else?"

"I don't know. She might. You can ask her anytime you want."

He wrote something in his notepad, walked to his car, grabbed a paper off the dash, came back, and handed it to me. It was the pictures I'd seen on the girl's individual flyers downtown, all squashed together in two rows. "Was the girl you saw in the back of his truck the night he vanished one of these girls?"

I scanned each face, but I tried my best not to look at them. The smiles, the eyes, the hope, the life. I knew I'd react and didn't want Morrell to read that reaction in my eyes, my soul. When I thought I'd scanned each square enough times, I told him I didn't know.

"Look again," he said. "Are you sure?"

I faked another long look at each and shook my head. "It's been so long. I can't be sure."

He took the paper back. Then he tossed out a bold, blunt question. "Did you have anything to do with these girl's disappearances or know who did?"

Luther, my conscience screamed. "No," I said. "Of course not."

"Why were you out at Plemons in the middle of the night?"

That question surprised me. It took me second to answer. "I drive around out there sometimes to clear my head. Why?"

"We have witnesses that said a truck matching the description of your Chevy was seen out there on private property, and that someone fitting your description was digging out there. And that just happened to be the day after the last Boulevard girl went missing."

"I wasn't digging anything anywhere. When I go out there, I roll down the windows and drive. I never even get out of my truck."

He glanced at his notes again like a lost man who needed help remembering what to say next. "We also have an officer report that says you were found out at a construction site, you know, the new school out at West Hill, late one night acting suspiciously." He flipped a page on the notepad, tapped it with his finger. "And that was the night after another girl went missing."

"What are you saying?" I asked with an edge of annoyance. He just stared at me.

"I have a lot of responsibility," I added. "I told that officer that sometimes I go out to the work sites at night to think things out. Set things up for the next day. So what? That makes me a killer?"

His eyes glued to mine, he licked his lips, and exhaled. I could smell his breath, and it was as stale and nondescript as his expression and clothing. "I didn't say that. Now don't get angry. You know I have a job to do just like you. I have to follow up on every lead." His eyes fell to his pad again. "So you're sure you don't know anything about what happened to those girls? Or if any one of them was the one you saw in the back of his truck?"

My eyes moved to the blue jays watching from the dead elm, listening, ready to tell Luther every detail of this conversation. "Positive," I insisted.

"Okay," he said flatly. He put his notepad away. "I might have more questions for you later, so don't stray too far from town."

His insinuation that I would stray told me everything I needed to know about how my answers had registered on his B.S. detector. "I won't," I said.

As he drove away, Brenda suddenly appeared by my side. She smelled sweet, like vanilla. "Was that Morrell?" she asked. I nodded. "What did he want?"

"To know if I'd seen anyone suspicious in the neighborhood lately. There's been a few garage break-ins this week and a bunch of tools were stolen."

She nodded, accepting the lie as easy as a dog accepts a treat. "How's your dad doing?"

"He's better," I said. "I talked him through the albums and now he's watching Clint Eastwood and eating burritos."

She laughed. "I think he eats twenty burritos a week."

I forced a smile and softly agreed.

"Well, I better get. I need to shower before *48 Hours Mystery* starts. I never miss that show."

I nodded. "Okay."

"I'll talk to you soon." She gave me a hug and headed home.

On the way to my truck, I glanced at the elm tree and noticed there was only one blue jay instead of two. Word of Morrell's suspicions would hit Luther's ear soon. I hoped he was happy with how I'd handled it.

Two blocks from my house I passed an unmarked Mercy Police cruiser that was heading the opposite direction. When I arrived home, Brianne didn't answer my calls in the house. Peering out the kitchen window, I saw her sitting on the back porch swing, her arms crossed over her belly, a pensive look on her face. I stepped outside and stopped beside the swing. A crisp breeze sliced through the air, swaying Sera's bird feeders. Moths swarmed the light above the back door. The bright halogen cut across the backyard, highlighting at least one blue jay in the tree.

"Are you all right?" I asked.

Startled, she jerked her face toward me.

"You feel okay?" I asked again. She'd had a touch of nausea and dizziness lately.

She broke eye contact and looked out across the yard. "Sergeant Adair came by here while you were gone."

The unmarked car. They'd been watching us, waiting for an opportunity to question us separately. Simultaneously.

"What did he want?"

"The cops think—"

My eyes shot to the bird perched in the tree, and I interrupted her. "Let's go inside." I didn't want Luther receiving a second report. Or third, if Brianne had talked to Adair outside. "Morrell came to my dad's and talked to me, too. Got my stomach in a knot. I need something to drink while we talk."

She looked up at me, and I reached for her hand. After a brief hesitation, she took it, and I helped her up and led her to the dining table in the kitchen. She asked for a glass of ice water, and I got myself a beer and sat across from her. There was a half-full mug of warm coffee on the table. Brianne had given up caffeine so Adair must've talked to her inside. Good. "What did Adair ask you?" I said.

She swirled her water, kept her eyes on the dancing ice. "If I've noticed any changes in your behavior in the past year or two."

"What did you tell him?"

"I told him that we'd talked about how distant you seemed after Randy's disappearance, how you spent a lot of time alone, but that you had gotten better since the wedding." She took a sip. "And I told him about EnviroTek because he asked how we could suddenly afford the Fit and our new house."

I took a pull and swished the cold beer around in my mouth to cut through the dry, caked saliva on my tongue. *Great. Now they'll start looking into EnviroTek. Fucking great.* "They think I have something to do with Randy's disappearance and maybe those Boulevard girls, too, huh?"

She nodded, looked up. "Do you?"

A swell of guilt rolled up my throat, and I swallowed hard to push it down. "No," I lied.

She took another sip of water. If she weren't pregnant and could smoke, she would've been chaining. "Adair said a lot of women on the Boulevard say they saw Randy down there all the time. With some of the missing girls even. Sometimes with another man who resembles you." She took another sip. "He thinks you and Randy might have had something to do with the first girl's disappearance, and then you guys got in a fight or something and you reported the body and got rid of Randy so you could lay the blame on him."

I smacked the table with my palm harder than I intended, startling her. "That's fucking stupid, Bri. I've never been down to the Boulevard looking for hookers with Randy. Ever. Besides, most of the girls have gone missing since Randy vanished, and they didn't even find the body in his truck. That means I would have to be the one to have kidnapped or killed all the girls since. If I planned on doing that, why would I have called them back then? That doesn't make any sense."

"Don't curse at me," she said with stern eyes. "I'm just telling you what he said."

I took a deep breath, pushed it out. "Do you believe him? Do you think I killed Randy? Do you think I kill hookers?"

She didn't hesitate. "No. I know you would never hurt anyone." Her eyes searched mine to let me know the statement came from her heart. God, I wanted to tell her the truth right then and there. About Luther. The birds. The notes. The sacks. Get it all off my chest. Share the burden that was driving me into the ground. I wanted her to feel sorry for me and for us to wake Sera and run and hide in some foreign country. Mexico maybe. But that couldn't happen. I pushed the urge to the corner of my mind and locked it away.

"What did Morrell say to you?" she asked.

"Basically the same. He asked if Randy and I went down to the Boulevard looking for hookers together, and where I was the night some of those girls went missing. And then he showed me some flyers and wanted to know if I recognized any of the girls." I took a huge gulp of beer. "When I told him I didn't, he got mad. Then when I asked why he suddenly thought all this about me, he said they got an anonymous tip that I was involved. Can you believe that? An anonymous fucking tip."

"Who do you think called?"

I took another long, slow drink, buying a little thinking time. Telling her I'd initially, briefly, thought it could have been her would not have been a good idea. Not with her pregnant and just having been questioned by the police. And telling her that my second thought was that it was her beloved brother Ryan might not be that smart either. She protected him to a fault, as if he were a helpless child that could do no wrong, wasn't accountable for his choices. But my assumptions would eventually come out, and I'd rather she heard them without Ryan there. Maybe she'd be less defensive. I swirled the liquid left in the bottle, finished it, and tossed the bottle in the trash. I tried to lay it on her easy. "I don't know if anyone did call. Maybe he made it up to see how I'd react since I was the last person seen with Randy. Cops can lie to you, you know?" I shrugged. "But if anyone did call, maybe it was Ryan."

"No way," she immediately responded. "He'd never do that. He would've come to me first." She glanced at her water, back at me. "Or he would've confronted you. You know he does that to people. He never holds his tongue."

The forceful tone in which she spoke, and the unwavering confidence in her eyes, told me to let it go. Retreat. At least I'd put it out there if later he admitted to it. I got another beer from the fridge and sat down. "Yeah. You're right. I just don't know who else it could be. The stuff the cops knew pointed at someone who knows me pretty well."

"Maybe it was someone you work with. Maybe one of those assholes you fired or something." She raised an angry finger in the air and widened her eyes. "Or maybe it was someone in Randy's family. Someone who knows you were the last person to see him."

"Maybe," I conceded.

We sat in silence for a short spell. A couple of awkward glances passed between us before I spoke again. "How are you feeling? You know, the nausea and all."

Her shoulders slumped with instant relief at the change of subject. "All right. When Adair came to the door I thought something terrible had happened to you and nearly vomited all over him." She chuckled, and so did I. "But I feel better now after talking to you."

I took her hand, squeezed it, and told her what she wanted to hear, needed to hear. "Everything's going to be all right. We'll be all right. I had nothing to do with any of this."

When Brianne went upstairs to take a bath, I snuck the rifle into the house and hid it in the garage, under a stack of scrap lumber. I loaded the 9 MM, left it under the seat in the Chevy, and then went to the back porch swing, where I sat and drank beer and shot the blue jays perched in the tree with my finger gun. I imagined they were the evil bird-cats in Lurth, the Featherlexes, beasts with tall pointy ears, four sharp claws, and a massive jagged wingspan, beasts that tried to sneak into houses through open windows and chimneys and steal children's pillows and blankets and toys to torment them. After I'd slaughtered a suitable amount of Featherlexes, I called Dad to make sure he was all right. He was watching another Eastwood flick and eating a popsicle.

Nineteen

Research, Sonogram, and a Name

Sera and I were on our way to the library when I first noticed the cops were keeping a close eye on me. An unmarked cruiser stayed five or six cars behind us the entire way there. I made a few irrational turns to confirm my suspicion, which brought bizarre looks from Sera, and the cruiser followed. When we parked and headed inside, the cruiser parked at the Sonic across the street. I couldn't tell who was inside, but I assumed Morrell had sent them to intimidate me, to let me know he was watching, not to really spy on me. They were too obvious. Besides, the Mercy Police Department didn't have enough manpower or money to spy on me twenty-four seven.

Sera had a book report due for history class, and one of the requirements was that they have at least two book sources. Her teacher, seventy-one-year-old Mr. Michael Hayes, Mr. Slenderman to the students because of his vicious criticism and long swooping limbs, was convinced the Internet was destroying the minds of the youth. He believed the information and misinformation on tap made them lazy, arrogant, and weak. That it was more confusing than helpful. I agreed with the confusing part. After I'd learned of Brianne's pregnancy, I'd done countless hours of online research and found it frustrating.

At night after Brianne had fallen asleep, and after I'd pulled the curtains closed to make sure the blue jays couldn't watch, I'd researched gifted humans, aliens, vampires—anything I thought might help me deal with Luther.

Like Mr. Hayes preached, the sites I searched contradicted

more than they agreed, confused more than they helped. According to some, vampires could die from a stake through the heart. One site said the stake had to be made of oak, but others said it had to be maple, or birch, or cedar. On a couple of other sites: no, all that's myth; stakes can't kill them; you have to chop off their heads like a zombie. Some sites said bullets couldn't hurt them, but others claimed silver bullets could damage them significantly. The whole garlic thing, not true. Or, wait, yes it is. And vampires could die from the sun, burst into flames and disintegrate into ashes the second a ray touched their skin, or, wait, no, that's bullshit, made up for movie vampires. I'd met with Luther in the daytime, so I knew the sun wouldn't disintegrate him. But as I looked back and thought about it, he did always make it a point to stay in the shade. In my car on the way to his cabin he'd leaned on the console, out of the sun, and on his cabin deck, he'd stayed in the shade of the trees. All the other times I'd been with him it had been night. So maybe the sun could hurt him, maybe weaken him anyway. Who knew?

If vampires didn't exist, and Luther was an alien, all bets were off. There are more sites and theories on aliens than anything else on the Internet. If he was from another planet or plane of existence, or if the real Luther had been taken over by a parasite alien, the possibilities were endless. Maybe he could regenerate limbs. Maybe he was more machine than man. Maybe there were thousands like him on our planet ready to converge on me and devour me in a cannibalistic feast. Maybe he couldn't die, or could live for thousands of years anyway. Or, hell, maybe a good sneeze, a simple germ, could kill him, like in *The War of the Worlds*.

Much like the alien angle, the gifted/supernatural angle sites gave endless, contradicting answers. Having watched *Heroes* and *X-Files* on Netflix while Brianne slept, and having devoured superhero comics as a child, I knew the possibilities were countless as the stars. There were gifted who could heal, fly, morph, were impervious, telekinetic, future seers, and on and on. And on and on. I knew Luther could read and channel emotions, talk to birds—his blue jays anyway—and that he could move faster than a normal human, but I wasn't sure about what else he could or couldn't do. To be honest, a part of me didn't want to know, either.

One night I also spent a few hours researching lavender, curious if the scent Luther carried had any significance to his being. All I found were hokey spiritual sites that claimed the scent promoted calmness, higher consciousness, inner peace, and symbolized a search for higher purpose, spiritual connectivity, or love. There was nothing about lavender related to powers or abilities. Maybe Luther thought it would help him seduce his victims, or calm them down, making it easier to kill them. Or maybe he just liked the smell. I don't know. Maybe it reminded him of his mom or the pond or something.

Sure to keep out of view from the blue jay perched in the pear tree outside the library window, I flipped through various books on beasts and monsters while Sera feverishly jotted down notes for her report. I watched the cruiser across the street and checked the blue jay more than I actually read, though. Like me, the bird seemed to occasionally check the cruiser. It flew over to the roof of Sonic a couple of times, staying for five or ten minutes before coming back.

In the silence of the library, I once again became all too aware of the invisible clock that was counting down to my unraveling, the numbers decreasing as steadily as water from a faucet. The cops were watching, following, pressing. The birds and Luther were watching, knew I was under suspicion. Ryan was "getting too close" to the truth. Although she tried to hide it, Brianne was still suspicious of me.

The clock was ticking, and there was only one way to stop it before it stopped me.

We left the library, and on the way to Brianne's doctor's office, Sera rambled on about her report and about how ridiculous Mr. Hayes was. As I listened, I constantly glanced in the rearview mirror but didn't see the cruiser following.

We parked next to Brianne's Fit, walked inside, and found her seated in the small waiting room. She had on her Golden

Corral clothes. Her sweaty hands were on her knees, and she had a nervous look in her eyes.

Sera sat between us and excitedly grabbed Brianne's hand. "Beth Anne said her mom knew she was going to be girl. She said she had a feeling that told her that only mothers can have. Do you have that feeling? What do you think the baby is? A boy or girl?"

Brianne glanced at me, then looked at Sera and shrugged.

"I hope it's a girl," Sera continued. "I've always wanted a little sister. Susie told me if you are carrying the baby in your back it's a boy, and if you carry it in the front it's a girl." Sera touched Brianne's belly. She had a tendency to be handsy like her mom. Always touching and hugging and leaning and rubbing. Esperanza had touched the head of any baby she crossed, the cheek of any kid she saw, and gently laid her fingers on every adult's hand she spoke with. She'd said it made people feel secure and special to be touched by someone who cared. "You haven't gotten much of a bump in front so it's probably a boy," Sera added. "I'd love to have a brother, too."

Brianne smiled and said she had no idea. She just wanted the baby to be healthy.

"Me, too," Sera said.

Before she could ask anything else, I asked Brianne, "Is Ryan coming?" She'd called him the night before to invite him. She'd invited her mom, too, but her mom had claimed to be ill.

Brianne shook her head. She looked like she was about to burst into tears. Taking a cue from Sera who was still holding Brianne's hand, I put my hand on Brianne's shoulder. She met eyes with me.

"I'm sorry," I said, figuring Ryan's no-show probably had something to do with me. Ever since our argument, he'd uncharacteristically avoided me at work, been short with me when he had to interact, and although he occasionally talked to Brianne on the phone, he hadn't been by the house once, increasing my belief that he was the one behind the anonymous call.

As we sat in the quiet waiting room, waiting for the doctor to call Brianne back, my eyes roamed to the parking lot outside, searching for an unmarked cruiser, and it occurred to me that maybe the cops had been keeping an eye on me for a long time. Maybe I'd only just noticed them. Maybe ever since—

"Brianne," Dr. Stevens' nurse called out from behind a partially opened door. She had a calm smile on her face and spoke soft and delicate. "Come on back." She led us to a room where Brianne changed into a gown and lay down on a table. I stood on one side of her, Sera, the other, holding her hand.

Dr. Stevens was sixty-something, six-foot-something, had silver hair, a tremulous left hand, and moved as delicately as his nurse spoke. First, he examined Brianne and listened to the baby's rapid heartbeat. Then he pulled the monitor close to the bed, slathered her belly with jelly, and began strobing the wand over her skin. Her free hand grabbed mine, tight. She hadn't said more than a handful of words since Dr. Stevens had entered the room. She'd been overly concerned with the health of the baby in the past few weeks, obsessively searching the Internet for birth defects, deficiencies, and diseases. We'd fought about it a couple of times, and I'd unwisely told her she might be the first person to have a baby damaged by the Internet. She hadn't talked to me for two days after that.

As Dr. Stevens moved the wand around, the shape of a curled, large-headed human became visible on the screen, eliciting a happy chirp from Sera. My heart sped up, and I smiled a gigantic smile. "There it is," Sera said. I glanced at Brianne and saw she had closed her eyes.

Dr. Stevens kept his eyes on the monitor. "Good size. Right on schedule. Looks healthy as we'd hoped for."

"Are the arms and legs there?" Brianne asked.

Dr. Stevens slid his eyes at her and smiled with one side of his mouth. "Yes." He patted her leg with his shaky hand. "Look for yourself. Everything looks great."

Brianne opened her eyes. Sera motioned at the monitor. "Look. There's the little person that's been making you have to pee all the time."

I ran my hand over Brianne's head, my thumb over the worry creases in her brow.

"Let's see if we can get a good angle..." Dr. Stevens said,

moving the wand a touch. "Ah, look." He pointed at a white smudge between the legs. "It's a boy."

I'd be lying if I said a profound feeling surged through me and changed the way I saw the world. Or if I said an immeasurable happiness overcame me. I *was* happy the baby was healthy. I *was* happy it was a boy. But Brianne's anxiety had more than half of my attention.

Sera squealed loud, and everyone looked at her. "Sorry," she said. "I couldn't help it. I'm going to have a brother!"

"Thank God," Brianne whispered, breaking her silence.

"I thought you didn't care if it was a boy or girl?" Sera asked.

"I don't," Brianne answered. "I'm just glad he's all there."

"He looks perfect," Sera said. "Right, Dad?"

"He does," I agreed.

Brianne was thirty weeks pregnant before she was willing to decorate the baby's room. We bought a crib and matching changing table/dresser from local Mercy carpenter Luke Knowles, who makes everything by hand and without toxic chemicals. It cost a pretty penny more than the snap-togethers at Mel's Furniture, but it's what Brianne wanted. Her fear of the baby being born with genetic deformities had morphed into us causing other deformities after the birth by exposing the baby to chemicals. BHT, BHA, phthalates, and all that jazz.

Luke brought the crib and dresser by on a Saturday, and the following morning Brianne and I were putting the final "boy" touches on the room. We used to mock our friends when they had a baby on the way and would decorate in the traditional blue or pink, sports and princesses, but when our turn came, we fell right in line with them. We joked about it all morning, like old times, her blaming me for our slip into mainstream, me blaming her.

Brianne's friends at the Golden Corral had had a baby shower for her the week before and had pitched in and bought a slew of diapers and onesies for her. She was folding the onesies and stacking them in the dresser, her round belly making it hard for her to reach the back of the open drawer, when she asked me to go get the rocking chair from the garage.

"All righty," I said.

"I think that's last thing we need to bring in and we'll be done." She stopped folding and glanced at me. "Then we can take a break and have some lunch."

"Pretty hungry, huh?" I asked.

"Starving."

"If you want, I'll go by Rosa's after I bring the chair up and get some of those chicken tacos you like."

She nodded and a soft smile stretched across her face. Like her breasts, her cheeks had plumped up in the last week or two, giving her face a round cherub quality. Keeping her eyes locked on mine, she dropped the onesies, walked over, knocked my lucky Ranger's hat off my head and kissed me, swirling her tongue around inside my mouth. She tasted sweet, like freshly squeezed orange juice mixed with vanilla ice cream, which she'd had for breakfast. She slid her hand down my abdomen and rubbed my crotch. "When's Sera supposed to be back?" she asked.

"Not until this afternoon," I answered, running my hand up under her shirt.

She grabbed one of my belt loops and led me to our room. Our sex life had always been healthy. No matter what else was going wrong in our life, the sex was always good. We often joked that our libidos had been separated at birth. But in the last month, our sex life had exploded from good to fucking awesome. Brianne seemed to want it all the time. Something about the pregnancy, maybe the hormones, I don't know, made her like a rabbit in heat. All I had to do was sneak my hand down her pants and squeeze her ass when no one was looking, or even just give her my best sexy wink, and she would start surveying the area, searching for the proper location to do the deed. She said her orgasms were more intense lately, longer too, and she wanted to get the most out of it before that baby reamed her. I was more than happy to oblige. I told her she could use me as her sex slave whenever she wanted.

When we finished, she hopped in the shower, and I dressed and headed downstairs to get the rocker. Storm clouds were brewing to the west of town, and I flicked on the TV as I passed through the living room to check the weather on the noon news. A tornado had skirted the north side of Mercy two weeks earlier, causing Brianne to demand we have a storm shelter installed in the backyard. A guy from Blankenship Tornado Safety was supposed to give us an estimate on Friday.

I found the rocker in the corner under a quilt. My dad had given us the hand-made rocker. It was the same one my mom had rocked me in. She called it our Lurth portal. "When I start rocking," she'd always said, "just close your eyes and hold on tight." Brianne and Sera had worked together and made some blue and white, back and seat cushions for the chair. Using the seat cushion to help balance the chair on my head, I had taken two steps upstairs when I heard Michelle Farmer, the same lady who'd reported on the missing Boulevard girls months earlier, talking about them again. My legs froze and all my after sex-giddiness disappeared. I turned and watched the screen.

"The number of the missing Boulevard women has now been reported by some people to be six or seven, all having gone missing in the past two years," Michelle said. "All of them are suspected to be prostitutes, and I found one woman who worked with them who was brave enough to talk to us."

The screen cut to what appeared to be a prostitute standing on the corner of Roosevelt and the Boulevard in front of the Night-Bye-Night Motel. Her face was blurred out and her voice distorted. She wore cut-off jeans and a sloppy tank. Sores and scabs dotted her visible arm. "All of us are scared of the Boulevard Monster," she said, her voice oddly as gruff as a man's. I wasn't sure if the media had altered it on purpose or her throat had been marinated in smoke and liquor for far too long. "Something nasty and evil is out here with us. We all feel it. It's scary to be out at night now. Dangerous. Even if you aren't working. That monster could be behind any dark corner waiting to snatch you. You never know." The woman shook her blurry head. "Those girls who went missing were just trying to make a living. Doing the best they could for themselves. They didn't deserve to be taken or killed."

"Have you seen anything suspicious in particular you can tell us about?" Michelle asked.

"Just shadows that I stay away from." The woman wiped at her blurry face with a blurry hand, then added, "Right now everything out here is suspicious. Rumors are flying like bats out of Hell. Everyone thinks they've seen him. Hiding. Waiting. Hating"

The screen cut back to Michelle Farmer in the studio. "I spoke to two other women off record, and they confirmed this woman's sentiment. Everyone walking the streets of the Boulevard for any reason is terrified. Rumors of the Boulevard Monster's identity are growing with no end in sight. I reached out to Detective Morrell at the Mercy Police Department for an interview, but he denied my request, saying the investigation was ongoing, and that the department is doing everything it can to find the missing girls, following up on every lead. If you have any information on the missing Boulevard women or the identity of the so-called Boulevard Monster, call Crime Stoppers." The number popped up on the bottom of the screen.

I hurried over to the TV and shut it off when I heard the floorboards in the upstairs hall creaking. Brianne stopped at the top of the stairs. She was drying her hair with one towel, another tied around her waist below her baby bump. "What are you doing?" she asked.

"I was just checking the weather and getting the rocker." I continued upstairs, suddenly feeling hot, flushed. Guilty as hell. "You want to ride to Rosa's with me?" I asked. She stepped out of my way, and I passed her without making eye contact.

"Sure. Let me get changed real fast."

As she dressed, I put the rocker where she wanted it, then went to the bathroom to splash cold water on my face, to rinse off the guilt. That was the first time I'd heard the name Boulevard Monster. It was a fitting name for Luther. I couldn't have come up with a better one myself.

Twenty

Goddamn Flyers

I wasn't sure if Luther hadn't contacted me because he knew the cops were watching or because he'd left town. My assumption was that he had "investors" in various cities in the U.S. and possibly all over the world. It would make sense. To keep suspicion at bay. He couldn't risk having too many women, prostitutes or not, vanishing all at once. But if a hooker vanishes here and there every now and then in one city, then a few others in another city halfway across the country, who would connect the dots? That would be typical run-of-the-mill occurrences. Often, sad as it sounds, a missing hooker in a large city is like a lost sock. You throw out a few possibilities of what could've happened to it and move on. I assumed this was why Luther vanished for months at a time. His reach was long. Web-like. Planned out to the T. He knew better than to stick around any one place for too long.

Either way, I was glad Luther hadn't contacted me. I'd had time to do more research, and time to assemble a killing kit. Despite how ridiculous it sounds, in a backpack in the garage I had three sharpened stakes, one made from oak, one from birch, and one from elm. I had a bottle of holy water I'd swiped from Saint Stephens on Western, a bulb of garlic, a crucifix, a large knife, a container of lighter fluid, and a box of waterproof matches. Overkill? Maybe. Paranoia? Definitely. But I had to be ready for anything. I still had the rifle in my garage, the handgun and a machete in my truck.

Time had also given my guilt time to fester. Every time I'd go baby shopping with Brianne, or to the mall with Sera, or to the grocery store, or to Lowe's for work supplies, I'd see the missing person fliers. One day, when no one was looking, I ripped one off a bulletin board and shoved it in my pocket. Before long, I had secretly swiped one of every missing Boulevard girl. At home, I studied them, memorized each missing girl's face, birthdate, likes and dislikes, and so on. I had no idea how many of them Luther had killed or how many I'd helped him dispose of, but I was certain I carried some of them to their final resting place.

Those missing girl's families deserved to give their loved one a proper burial and send-off. I couldn't imagine if anything like that happened to Sera. If she went missing and I...I don't want to type about that. The thought alone is unbearable.

I kept the flyers in an old orange and red folder. I hid it on a shelf in the closet in the unused spare bedroom, under a box that held my childhood baseball card collection. The room was littered with unpacked boxes and unused furniture. We called it the Give Away Room. When home alone, I'd go to the room, lock the door, pull the blinds closed (to keep the birds' eyes off me), and study the flyers, giving the girls my attention, learning who they were, where they were from. I hoped wherever they were, whatever form they were in in the afterlife, that they knew I was sorry for my role in their deaths, and that I cared about who they'd been.

One Monday after work I went to Wizzards and knocked back four shots of whiskey and three Dos Equis. Brianne was working the night shift and wouldn't be home to keep an eye on me. The pregnancy had made her extremely horny, but it had also made her frown on my drinking more than ever. I'd been hiding it by drinking Vodka at home instead of beer. The beer odor was hard to mask, took hours to consume, the cans and bottles hard to hide. But I could hide a bottle of Vodka behind the towels on the top shelf in the spare bathroom that Brianne rarely used, take a couple of swigs when I went to pee, pop a peppermint in my mouth on my way back downstairs, and be on my merry way. I just had to be sure not to kiss Brianne for a while afterward. Detective Morrell's bullshit detector had nothing on hers.

Tipsy and guilt-ridden when I got home from Wizzards that Monday night, I went upstairs, opened the door to the Give Away Room, and found Ryan standing in front of the closet, rifling through my flyers. He hadn't been to our house in months as far as I knew.

"What the hell are you doing?"

He jerked his head my way, flinched back and tripped over a stack of CDs. I flicked on the light to brighten the room as he caught his balance. He peered at me with surprised yet challenging eyes, like a coyote caught in the chicken coop, feeling no remorse because it was starving.

"What are these?" he asked, jiggling the flyers.

I stepped toward him. How dare he. Dumbass. I motioned at the flyers. "Why are you snooping through my shit? How long have you been here? How did you get in?"

"Why do you have them?"

"That's none of your business."

"None of my..." He shook his head seemingly in disgust. "I know why you have them."

"Oh yeah, Sherlock. You know everything, don't you?"

He glanced at the flyers, back at me. "You're involved with the disappearance of these girls."

I didn't answer.

"It all fits." His grip tightened on the flyers, twisting them into a crumple. "Randy's weird disappearance. The change in your personality. The new money. The blood on your hands that one night. Going out to Plemons and digging." A pause. "Someone's paying you to do it, huh?"

I forced out a raspy, nervous chuckle that sounded like PVC pipe clacking together. "You've seen one too many movies, man."

"You know I'm right."

"No, I don't."

"Yeah, you do."

"First off," I said, "why would I call the cops about the body in Randy's truck if I was involved? That would be fucking stupid."

He'd thought about this a lot, had an answer ready to leap off the tip of his tongue. "To blame him. I think he was helping you and you either got scared he would talk, or you got greedy and wanted all the money for yourself."

"Did Morrell feed you that bullshit? How many times have you talked to him?" I pushed a frustrated breath. "The money is from an investment. I told you that, remember?"

"Then how come I couldn't find any information about EnviroTek online?" A pause. His eyes were full of *that's-right-I-researched-it* pride. "And how come the guy I talked to at Brewer's Investment Services hadn't heard of it? If it was such a huge international success you'd think more people would know about it. Or it would at least have a fucking website."

"I can show you the check stubs if you want. The tax forms." My voice cracked, sounded weak. "And the blood on my hands that night was from..." I held my hands out then swiped them through the air as if scattering a fart cloud. I wanted to lash out at him for following me, spying on me, for endangering himself and our family. "Forget it," I said. "I told you what that was from. You can believe me or not. I don't care."

He jiggled the flyers again. "Why do you have these if you don't have anything to do with it? Most normal people don't have a stack of these flyers hidden in their house."

"They weren't hidden."

"Does Brianne know about them?"

I looked toward the large window facing the backyard. The blinds were open. Two blue jays were on the ledge outside, watching, listening, as usual. Fuck. My eyes swiveled to Ryan's. "Maybe I feel guilty because one of them was the one I found in Randy's truck. Maybe I could've stopped him or something. It eats away at me every fucking day."

"You're lying. Most of these girls went missing after he vanished. And since then, you've gotten richer and richer, shadier and shadier. But," he chuckled, "I bet you'll say that's just a coincidence, huh?"

I marched forward, kicked a cardboard box filled with clothes aside, and stopped two feet in front of him. "Tell me something," I said. "How long have you been spying on me? Are you the one that called the cops?" I threw up finger quotes. "Anonymously."

Apprehension flashed across his eyes.

"I thought you said we could talk about *anything*," I said. "Why didn't you just ask me about it if we're supposed to be so close?"

He stayed silent. Sweat beaded up on his temples. I snatched the flyers out of his hand. Some ripped in two, and he dropped the remnants and raised his fists head-high, fight-high. "Why didn't you just tell me that you..." he trailed off, shaking his head.

"Tell you what?" I asked, and tapped his bony chest with a stiff finger. "You better mind your own business and stop snooping around my fucking house before I—"

"Before you what? Make *me* vanish like Randy?"

Slow, silent seconds unwound. I eyed the watchful birds, trying to decide what to do. When I finally glanced at Ryan's hands, I smirked. "Maybe I will. What are you going to do about it?"

He hit me square in the nose. Not hard enough to knock me down, but hard enough to sting like a son-of-a-bitch and blur my eyes. I immediately tossed my lucky Rangers cap aside and swung back, landing my knuckles on the side of his head. He growled and tackled me to the ground, and we wrestled into the doorway.

"You're a stupid paranoid snooping son-of-a-bitch," I yelled as I tried to squirm out from under him, blocking his blows with my forearms. I managed to get a hold on both his wrists and thrust him out into the hall. Then I lunged at him as he crab-walked backwards toward the stairs. I landed on his legs and felt his ankle twist at an awkward angle under my weight. He moaned in pain, and I struggled to straddle his waist as he kicked and swung. He landed two blows to my face before I finally hit back. I hit him once in the chest, and once in the face, bloodying his nose. His fighting slowed then, and I thought he was about to give up, but then I felt a sharp pain in my arm, a pain that seemed to reach down to the bone. I screamed, and when I looked at my arm, I saw Ryan's pocketknife sticking out of the flesh like a flagpole sticking out of the ground. As I pulled it out and blood ran down my arm, Ryan sledge-hammered me in the chest with both hands, knocking me back. Then he wiggled out from under me and headed downstairs. I chased after him.

Looking back at me, he tripped on the second to last step and rolled into the front foyer. When he stood, he spun around and held his fists head-high like he had upstairs in the Give Away Room. He had a trail of thick blood running from his nose, and he was favoring the ankle that had twisted.

Cupping my hand over the stab wound, I stared at him. We were both panting, both unwilling to flinch. We'd been in a couple of tussles before. Usually when we were drunk. I'd blacked his eye once, and he'd repaid the favor years later. But we'd never fought like this. We were both brimming with anger. He thought I was a murderer. I thought he was stupidly sacrificing himself to an evil he didn't understand.

"Why the hell did you stab me?" I asked.

He didn't answer. At least not with words. He attacked me, swinging his arms like a flailing bird that was struggling to stay afloat after being shot. I backed up and fell onto the stairs. He kicked at me with his good foot, but I caught his leg and easily twisted him to the floor. His shoulder smacked the hardwood with a sickening thud. He struggled to pull his leg from my grip, causing me to fall to a knee and let go. He dove at me and was furiously swinging when Sera opened the front door.

She dropped her purse and screamed, "What are you guys doing?"

I looked her way, and Ryan cold-cocked me in the chin and my lights dimmed. When my eyes refocused, Sera was trying to pull Ryan off of me. He shoved her away, and she fell over her purse and squealed when she hit the ground. Ryan paused for a moment, realizing what he'd done, and went over to console her.

"I'm sorry, Sera," he said, reaching out for her arm. She jerked it away as I was getting to my feet.

"What's wrong with you?" she asked, her voice shaky, eyes shimmering with tears.

"Nothing...I...I'm sorry," Ryan said.

I grabbed him by the back of the shirt and threw him into

the coat rack by the open front door. The rack snapped in the center and coats and hats fell to the ground in a heap around him. When I stepped forward and reared back to punch, Sera grabbed my arm and said, "Dad, don't. Stop. Please. Stop." She was crying hard now. "Stop fighting."

I lowered my arm.

She put her head on my shoulder and cried and mumbled something I didn't understand. I wrapped my arm around her as Ryan rose and made his way out onto the porch. Two blue jays, probably the two that had been on the windowsill upstairs, were on the front lawn facing the doorway.

"Get out of here before I go get my gun," I yelled as Ryan dabbed blood from his nose with his shirt and limped onto the sidewalk leading to the road.

"Dad!" Sera squeezed my arm. "Stop!"

Ryan stared at us for a second before walking away.

Sera asked me what was going on, what we were fighting about, three or four times before I looked away from the birds and into her giant emotion-filled eyes. "Are you all right?" I asked. "Are you hurt?"

She shook her head. "I'm fine."

I ran my hand through her curls. "Are you sure?"

She nodded. "Why were you guys fighting?"

I didn't answer. I couldn't. I kissed her on the head, told her to lock the door behind me, and left as she pleaded for me to stay.

Twenty-One

Collier Kids Always Stick Together

I drove all over Mercy looking for Ryan.

I checked his apartment, Wizzards, the other bars and fast-food joints he frequented, a couple of his old girlfriend's places. I even cruised up and down the Boulevard a few times, a place I'd avoided like the plague ever since learning the cops were watching me. I drove for hours, stewing in the tense silence of my cab, sweating, constantly checking the rearview mirror to make sure no cruiser was tailing me. I was terrified the birds had already delivered the news of the fight to Luther, and he'd already taken swift action to get rid of Ryan.

When I arrived home a little after midnight and found Brianne sitting at the dining table still in her work clothes, her giant belly pressed against the table's edge, worry-creases lining her forehead, holding a mug of cold tea face-high and staring at it as though she'd been frozen mid-drink, I knew the one place I didn't check was the first place I should've.

Ryan had gone to the Golden Corral to tell Brianne everything. Of course. Why the hell hadn't I gone there first? Growing up, they'd only had one another, and when trouble arose for Ryan, he ran to Brianne for help. "Collier kids always stick together," he and she had said to me many times over the years. They always said it in unison with childish grins plastered on their faces and their arms looped around one another's necks, too. If they sided against me when it came to small things like what food to pick up for dinner or what movie to rent, that's when it would happen. And when they said it, you could see how they took pride in the words, felt a sense of strength behind them, a connection that would always be there. I should've known he'd go to her first.

I pulled out a chair and sat across from her. She didn't look at me or lower her mug. "Where's Sera?" I asked.

Long seconds passed before she blinked and took in a loud breath, like she'd suddenly been plugged in and turned on. She lowered the mug and met eyes with me. "She's asleep."

"Is she all right?"

"She's upset. Scared and confused."

I took off my lucky Ranger's cap, set it on the table, ducked my head, and ran my hand over the stubble. "I take it you already talked to Ryan?"

"Yep," she said with conviction. Like she already had a solid grasp of the absolute truth.

I lifted me head. "Where is he now?"

"I don't know." By the look in her eyes, I knew she wouldn't tell me even if she did know.

"Do you even want to hear my side of it?"

"It would help me understand what's going on with you." A beat. "If you would tell me the truth for once."

"The truth? You want the truth." I glanced at the kitchen window and saw a blue jay perched on Sera's PAUL bird feeder, watching, listening. I put my hand on my lucky Rangers cap and squeezed it. I didn't know what the truth was anymore. There was my truth, the Luther truth, a truth eating away at me like termites on untreated wood, and then there was the truth everyone else knew, the truth I had to maintain and repair like the upkeep on a crumbling house. It was getting harder and harder to keep the house standing, but I had to try. For a little longer. For her sake. "The truth is that I found Ryan snooping around in the house when I got home."

"I gave him a key, and he can come here any time he wants," she shot back. "Why do you have those flyers hidden up there in that closet?"

The stern change in her tone when she asked the question led me to believe she thought she already knew the answer, and it didn't favor me. I knew Ryan had told her his theory on why

I had them. I figured he'd been feeding her many of his theories about me for months. And I figured that she'd bought most of them hook, line, and sinker. Still, I told her the same lie I'd told Ryan. "I felt guilty about that girl I found in Randy's truck. What if he was responsible for some of the other girls, too? I should've seen it. Maybe I could've saved some of them."

The doubt in her eyes never faltered. She didn't buy it. I like to believe part of her wanted to, the part that wanted the father of her child to be a good man, but she didn't.

"You don't believe me?" I asked.

"What about the blood on your hands and all over your shirt that one night?"

I put my lucky Ranger's cap back on. "It was an accident. I told you, I hit a dog."

She lowered her mug. "Ryan said he saw you sneaking around a construction site one night, and that you got mad when he found you and you swung a shovel at him and threw a beer bottle at him. Is that true?"

"I went out there to think. I was stressed about work. You know how Dan is, how I get." I shook my head. "I swung the shovel and threw the bottle because he was drunk and being an asshole."

Her eyes held steady. "He also said he followed you out to Plemons after that and saw you digging with a shovel. What were you doing out there?"

"I went out there to be alone after we got in that shovel-fight. I wasn't digging, though. I don't know why the hell he said that."

"He saw you, Seth."

"I wasn't digging. I don't know what else to tell you."

"Tell me the truth."

"I'm trying. You just seem to already have your mind made up so what's the point. You always believe him over me. Always have, always will."

She wrapped both her hands tightly around her mug and leaned forward as far as her belly allowed. "I only believe him over you when his story makes more sense than yours."

I glanced at the window and saw two birds now, one on each

feeder. They almost seemed eager to tattle. To let Luther know Brianne was getting close, too. I slid my eyes back to Brianne's belly, then up to her eyes. "You really think it makes sense that I've been lying about investing in EnviroTek? That our money is coming from somewhere else? That I'm working for the mob or some shit like that, like Ryan thinks?" She just stared. "You think it makes sense that I have those flyers because I killed those girls or something? Like trophies? You think that blood on my hands was from a kill? You think I called the cops on Randy to get him to take the fall? After all these years, you think any of that makes sense when it comes to me? Do you have any idea how ridiculous that sounds?"

"I know that even though you've been trying real hard to act normal, you've changed since Randy vanished. At first I thought you were cheating. Especially before the wedding, remember? But now..." She looked down into her mug.

I slammed my hand down onto the table, and her eyes shot up at mine. "Now what? What?!"

She didn't answer.

"You're just regurgitating Ryan's bullshit theories. Do you have any thoughts of your own on this?"

After a long pause during which the only sounds were our alternating breaths and the ticking of the kitchen clock, she said, "Where'd you get the envelope full of cash at the wedding?"

I'd forgotten all about that, but Ryan hadn't. "It was a bonus from the guys at EnviroTek. I told Ryan that, but I guess he didn't believe me. So I guess you don't either."

"Why didn't you tell me about it? Why didn't you introduce me to the other investors at the wedding?"

"Didn't Ryan *tell* you? They didn't come to the wedding. I found it in the mailbox on my way out of the house before the ceremony, and by the time the wedding was over it had slipped my mind. Remember all the cash we spent on our honeymoon? That was it. Happy?" I sighed. "Jesus-fucking-Christ, Bri. Ryan has your head running in paranoid circles. This isn't good for the baby. I swear to God if anything happens to you or the baby because he's doing this shit to us I'll...I'll..."

Her eyes began to well up. "It's not just him. Or your

behavior. It's the cops, too. They think you're involved way more than what you say. Why would they think that? Why do they keep coming back and talking to me and Ryan? Why do they sometimes park down the street and watch the house? What do they know, Seth?"

"I thought they only came to talk to you once. Adair. When Morrell came and talked to me."

"Morrell came to my work and talked to me two other times, and he came here a couple of weeks ago. I just didn't tell you."

"Why? Because you didn't want to upset me? Or because you believe their bullshit?"

The way she looked at me gave me the answer I'd hoped wasn't there but deep down knew was. She believed some of the cops and Ryan's suspicions. She believed I was involved somehow, someway. Smart girl. But too smart for her own good. She had no idea the consequence of seeing my truth, knowing my truth. If she did, she would've been smart enough to turn a blind eye.

"I don't want you getting upset," I said. "It's not good for you or the baby." I tried to touch her hand, but she pulled back. "I don't know what else to tell you. I've given you all the truth I can." I stood up, walked to the back door, and when I glanced back over my shoulder, she was staring blankly at the mug again, like she'd been unplugged.

For the millionth time I wanted to run over and hug her and tell her everything. How scared I was. How sorry I was. How much I loved her and Sera and the Ryan and the baby. I swallowed down all the emotion that came along with the thought in a loud, dry gulp and headed to the Chevy.

When I opened the driver's door, a blue jay swooped down and dropped a note on the hood. My gut knotted up as I picked up the note.

Ryan's too close.

I hated Luther's perfect fucking fancy handwriting. I wadded up the note and hurled it. The blue jay swooped down, plucked it off the ground, and disappeared into the night. Another one followed me as I drove away.

Twenty-Two

Only Pussies Can't Make Decisions, Boy

After driving around for a while to make sure I wasn't being followed by the cops, I drove to our latest construction site—a two-story ranch house and accompanying barn two miles past the BNSF station, south of Mercy. After parking and rolling down the windows, I sat in the Chevy with my 9MM on my lap. I knew I didn't have much time, but I couldn't make up my mind about the Ryan situation, didn't feel confident on any single line of action.

As I sat there debating, worrying, waffling, watching the blue jays in the red oaks lining the dirt road leading to the house, something my dad had told me when I was a teen came to mind, the message coming across so loud and clear it was as though he were sitting next to me, whispering it in my ear.

My sophomore year my baseball coach, Coach McKinney, had been riding my ass about my grades (All C's except English where I had an A), and he'd been threatening to suspend me from the team anyway ever since me and Jack Simmons had been caught drinking in the alley behind Moore's Pharmacy. I was a better than average player but knew baseball wasn't a real future for me. I did it because I thought my dad wanted me to, no other reason.

When I went to my mom for advice on whether I should quit or not, she sent me to my dad. He said, "You're a young man now. It's your decision." I said, "I don't know what to do, though." He shook his head and looked at me with disdain, the way he often did when he was blistering drunk. Like I wasn't worthy to be in his presence, to be his son. "Only pussies can't make decisions, boy," he said, then walked away. "Man up," I heard him yell just before he slammed the garage door. I quit the next day, and that was the last time in my life I asked for his advice.

Luther would take swift action against Ryan. He didn't take well to uninvited intrusions on his world. I couldn't just let it happen. I couldn't let Ryan go through what the naked Colorado man had. I was the one who had fucked up and allowed him to get close to the truth. Ryan's only mistake was being too damn observant. And nosy. And caring. But to Luther, he was bothersome. He was nothing. He was a stain that needed to be cleansed before it ruined the fabric permanently.

Running my finger up and down the 9 MM's barrel, I watched the birds watch me and made a decision—a decision that I will regret and not regret, as odd and unexplainable as that sounds, until the day I die. I didn't know exactly how things would turn out with Luther or Ryan, or Brianne, Sera, the baby, or Dad for that matter, but I had to make a decision. I had to man up. I couldn't let Luther dictate the fate of my family any longer. I couldn't let him decide when and how Ryan would die.

I shoved the gun under the seat, took a scrap of paper and pencil out of the glove box, and wrote a message to Luther. My handwriting looked elementary to his, all uneven and sloppy, and I was certain he would chuckle at it, see it as a sign of my weakness, his superiority. With my eyes locked on the closest blue jay, I held the note out the open window, whistled, and shook it. When the bird landed atop the side-view mirror, I said, "Take this to your leader, shithead." Then I laughed a maniacal laugh that I didn't know was coming, and I'm sure frightened all the wildlife in the area. It felt good to let it out, though. Refreshing. Like a floodgate inside me had been opened, releasing a torrent of pinned-up tension.

The decision was made. There was no turning back. And there was a strange mixture of fear and relief accompanying that.

Twenty-Three

Of Monsters and Men

The note I wrote Luther asked him to please meet me at the ranch house south of Mercy before sunrise, and to please not do anything to Ryan until we talked. I added that Ryan was family. Like a real brother. No matter how callous and reptilian and self-serving Luther was, I assumed he remembered the pain associated with losing a brother based on what he'd told me that night in Colorado. That was one of the few times I'd seen real emotion in his eyes. I hoped calling Ryan my brother would touch on that sensitive nerve, and he'd decide to hear me out before taking care of Ryan. I signed the note, Your friend, Seth.

Friend—I hoped that would help, too. He seemed to like calling me that.

I kept the 9 MM on my lap and both windows down while I waited. I wasn't sure how long it would take Luther to arrive, but I figured if he planned on killing Ryan, it wouldn't be long.

I was right. He appeared behind the row of red oaks lining the dirt road that led to the ranch house less than an hour after the blue jay took my note. I watched him move toward the Chevy, his legs and arms gliding beneath his Guayabera and slacks effortlessly, as though he were made of liquid. That wide, cocky unbreakable smile was on his face as he opened the passenger door and slid into the truck without making a sound. His eyes fell to the gun on my lap, then rose to mine as the smell of lavender consumed the cab.

"You going to shoot me?" he asked.

I lay my hand on the gun. "Would it work?"

His head tilted back and a raucous laugh bellowed from his mouth. Once his laughter faded, he slapped my thigh, and my grip tightened on the gun. "Good one," he said, then gestured at my hand. "You need to relax, friend. You're going to give yourself an aneurysm." He held his hand in the air and wiggled his lithe fingers, reminding me he could induce relaxation anytime I wanted. "I could help you out you know."

I shook my head. "It's kind of hard to relax when..." I looked away.

"When your brother-in-law has to die?" he filled in.

I could tell by his tone that his smile was gone. I nodded, took off my lucky Rangers cap, ran my hand over head.

"You don't have to worry about it, though," Luther said. "I'm going to take care of it for you. You don't have to see anything. You can pretend he was in trouble with the government and went to live in the Bahamas or something. The imagination can be a beneficial tool if you use it right. I've been using that trick for longer than I can remember."

I put my hat back on. "It's not that simple." I took in and forced out a deep breath. "I...I..." I could feel water building in my eyes, a lump forming in my throat.

"It is that simple."

Slowly, I moved my eyes to his. "I saw the terror in that guy's eyes in Colorado. I've seen the terror frozen on the faces of some of the...the people in the...the...the...sacks I've buried. I don't want Ryan to experience that terror. He doesn't deserve it. I'm the reason he's in this situation. He's done nothing wrong. He was simply smart enough to catch on to the mistakes I've made."

"The guilt's getting to you, isn't it?"

"It's eating a hole right through my chest," I said.

"I get it. I've been there." Luther slid his eyes across the horizon. "So what is it you want to do with him then? We can't let him—"

"I want to do it myself," I cut in. "I want to kill him." A tear fell from my eye.

Luther shook his head. "That's not a good idea. How's that

going to alleviate any of your guilt? It'll make it worse if you kill him."

"I've already killed him anyway, haven't I?" I bit my lip, lightly shook my head. "I don't want him being horrified in his last moments. I don't want him to see it coming. If you come at him, he'll see it coming." I wiped the wet off my cheek. "I know it sounds selfish, but I want to make amends with him before he goes. We've been fighting a lot lately, and I'll feel better knowing we were good before he..."

Luther remained still and silent for a long while. I don't think he saw my request coming. I don't think he thought I had it in me to kill. "How do you want to do it?" he eventually asked.

"I figured I'd tell him I want to drive out to Plemons and have a few beers and talk things out."

"You think he'll agree to that."

"I used to take him out there to ride dirt bikes when he was a teenager. I think he'll agree to go with me if I remind him of all the good times we had out there. It's a place where we bonded. The place where we shared our first beer together. Where we talked about things we couldn't in front of Brianne. Tits and blow jobs and porn. In a way, the riverbed out at Plemons is to us what the pond where you and your brother hung out was to you."

Luther nodded.

"Ryan's got a big heart, and I believe he loves me like a brother, too. I think he'll give me a chance to explain."

"How do you plan on killing him?"

"I'll..." My voice cracked, and I cleared my throat. "I'll wait until he goes to take a piss or turns his back to me or something and I'll just... you know." I lifted the gun off my lap. "In the back of the head."

"You sure?"

I nodded as an image of Ryan collapsing with a hole in his head and a smile on his face flashed across my mind's eye. "My hope is that we'll have made up, and he'll die happy and never see it coming."

A quirky smile crossed Luther's face. "Like in that book about that retarded guy who loves rabbits and his friend shoots him?"

"Right," I said. I knew the book, had read it in high school my junior year. I hadn't made the connection, though. "But Ryan's far from retarded. He's got a quick wit."

"Which is why you'll have to be very careful how you do it. You'll have to make sure no one else is around. Have a hole already dug. An alibi for when the cops come asking about him. When Brianne does."

"I will."

"He thinks you're a murderer or working for one so you'll have to be very convincing in your explanation about what's been going on, too."

"I will."

"You can't be emotional. You can't be hesitant. You can't be scared. You can't allow the guilt to break you. You can't mention the real truth." Luther counted these statements out on his fingers.

I looked at the blue jay that was standing on the hood of my truck like a hood ornament, then at the group of them clustered around the red oaks lining the dirt road. "I won't," I said. "I owe him that much."

After a long silent stretch, I asked, "Will you let me do it? Please."

Luther smiled and put his hand on my shoulder. I worked hard not to flinch, but must've anyway. "Don't worry," he said. "I'm not going to do anything to you unless you want me to."

"I don't," I said, glancing at his hand. "I don't deserve to feel relaxed right now."

Luther removed his hand. "When you kill him, I will be there, though."

Just what I figured he'd say. "You don't think I can handle it? You think I'll fuck it up?"

"No. I like to think of it as supporting you in your time of need."

"I can handle it," I said.

"And I'll let you handle it. But I will be there just in case. I have a lot at stake here, too. Remember? This isn't just your dilemma. Ryan has put a very uncomfortable thorn in my side." He opened the truck door and stepped out. "You have twenty-four hours to get this done, or I will do it myself." He slammed the door. "My way."

"How will you know when I'll be there?"

He looked at me hard, like he couldn't believe I'd asked the question. Like I should already know the answer. And I did: the birds.

"Right," I said, my eyes moving to the hood ornament bird. "Your pals."

He smiled, shut the door, and glided away as effortlessly as when he'd arrived. When he passed the red oak trees and dirt road, I yanked my binoculars out of the glove box. Beyond the tree line was forty acres of flat plain. I wanted to see where he was going, *how* he was going, but in the few seconds it took to grab the binoculars and put them to my eyes and focus, he was gone.

Twenty-Four

Bathroom Talk

I didn't sleep a wink that night and left for work early, before Brianne and Sera woke up, hoping to talk to Ryan and start buttering him up before the workday started. Sitting in my truck, I watched the oak tree-lined dirt road until a little after eight, watched all the other guys file in, but Ryan never arrived. After I gave instructions to the rest of the crew, I tried Ryan's cell a couple of times, but he didn't answer, and I didn't bother leaving a message.

A few hours later, while we were preparing the rounded back porch for cement, I glanced at the dirt road and I saw Dan's truck approaching, kicking up dust. He pulled up twenty yards from where I stood and motioned me over. When I reached the driver's side window, he wedged his diet soda between his thighs and greeted me with: "What the hell's up between you and Ryan?" He'd gained at least another forty pounds over the past year, and his hair had continued to rapidly abandon his scalp.

"What do you mean?"

"He called me this morning and said he quits. When I asked why, he said it was because of you. That he couldn't work with you anymore." He slurped his soda. "So what's going on? I thought you two were thick as thieves?"

I put my hand on my hips. "We had an argument this weekend."

"About what?"

"I don't know. Stupid family shit. We both had one too many

beers and before I knew it we were on the ground wrestling and calling each other names. Don't worry, it'll blow over. We've had tons of fights like this, and everything always turns out fine. Give him a break. I'm sure he'll show up tomorrow."

"Just because he's kin to you doesn't mean he gets special fucking privileges. He quit." His wide eyes locked on mine, he slurped long and loud.

I glanced at the blue jay on a nearby front loader, back at Dan. I could tell by Dan's expression that he wanted me to beg. He wanted me to stroke his ego, acknowledge that he was in charge. "Please, Dan," I said. "I'll go talk to him after work and patch things up. He needs this job."

Dan cranked his A/C up a notch and put the truck in gear. "If he doesn't show up tomorrow, he can't come back ever."

I patted Dan's beefy arm. "Thanks, Dan. I'll take care of it."

As he pulled away, he said, "And you better finish that back porch today. I've got the sprinkler guys coming to start piping tomorrow and I don't want you in their way."

I held up an acknowledging hand. He hit the brakes. "Make sure that detached garage roof is done, too," he hollered. "It should've been done last week."

"Will do," I said, wishing I could kick him in the teeth.

Ten minutes later, I put Tim Matthews in charge of the porch project, Roger Ogg in charge of the garage roof, and I left.

The twenty-four-hour window Luther had given me was closing fast.

Ryan's little Toyota was under the carport at his apartment complex. I grabbed my backpack, slung it over my shoulder, and hurried to his door. The blinds in the window to the right of the door were closed. The light above the door was off. I put my ear to the door and heard voices, TV voices, a commercial about used cars. I banged five hard times, waited a minute, then banged five more and called out Ryan's name. A few seconds later, the door cracked open, but just a bit. Ryan was in boxers, his hair disheveled, close-set eyes bloodshot from fatigue. His ankle was wrapped with an ace bandage.

"What do you want?" he asked.

"I want to talk to you about last night."

"I don't want to talk to you."

"Just let me come in for a few minutes. I feel bad about how everything went yesterday." He stared at me. "I'll answer all your questions honestly," I added. "No bullshit."

He looked me up and down. "Shouldn't you be at work?"

"When you didn't show up this morning and Dan told me you'd quit, I wanted to come and hash this out. I don't want you giving up your job because of me. And I sure as hell don't want you thinking I'm some kind of psychotic killer." I looked down at my feet, then back up. "We're family, man. Brothers. A few minutes is all I'm asking for and then I'll leave. Please."

"What's the backpack for?"

"There's something in it that I need to show you," I said.

He just stared at me, wanted more.

"I put it in the backpack because it's easier to carry that way. You know, since my arm has a knife hole in it." I gave him an ornery smile in an attempt to break the tension, to let him know I held no grudge, that I thought of our fight as another one of our scuffle stories we'd laugh about over a beer in a year or two.

Following a long pause, he slowly opened the door. Thank God. Step one was complete. I was inside the apartment. Now I had to drop the hammer.

I sat on the end of the couch closest to the door and put the backpack between my legs. He left the room for a moment, and when he limped back, he had on a White Zombie T-shirt and a giant hunting knife in his hand. He lit a cigarette and sat on the opposite end of the couch. He set the knife next to an ashtray on the end table beside him. "Well," he pushed out in a plume of smoke. "Talk."

I glanced at the door and noticed it wasn't locked. When I stood to lock it, Ryan asked what I was doing but I didn't answer. I peeked out the blinds behind the couch and saw a blue jay in a cottonwood in front of the apartment building. Another one was hopping along the top of my truck. I made sure the blinds were fully closed, then did the same for the kitchen window blinds, and the window in Ryan's bedroom. When I went back to the living room, I stopped in front of the TV. *The Price is Right* was on, a fat lady spinning the giant beeping number wheel.

Ryan's eyes squinted in confusion as I turned the volume up to an uncomfortable level. I made my way back over to the couch, and he took a hard drag from his smoke. "What's wrong with you?" he asked. "Are you on something?"

My eyes moved from Ryan, to the blinds, to my backpack. Once the words fell out of my mouth, there would be no turning back. A rejuvenating jolt of adrenaline and fear surged through me and my stomach fluttered. I met eyes with Ryan. He had no idea what was coming. No idea the weight of the hammer I was about to drop on him. But if anyone could bear the burden of my truth's weight, anyone who would saddle up next to me and attack the challenge head-on, it was Ryan Patrick Collier.

I picked up the backpack. "Come to the bathroom with me."

Ryan snuffed out his cigarette. "What for? You need help wiping your ass?"

"Just come on. Please."

He dropped his eyes to the backpack. "What's in there?"

"I'll show you in the bathroom."

His eyes slid to mine, and he slowly picked up his hunting knife, gripping it tight. He stood up, looked at the blaring TV, toward the bathroom, back at me. He pointed at the backpack with his knife. "What's in there? A gun?"

I held out the backpack. "You carry it," I said. "And look," I tossed the backpack onto the couch and lifted my shirt and spun around. "I don't have any weapons on me. I just want to talk." A beat. "Please. I need your help."

I went to the bathroom and turned on the shower and sink water full blast. My paranoia knew no bounds. A few seconds later, Ryan came in carrying the backpack and sat on the toilet lid. I closed the door, splashed a handful of cold water on my face, and told Ryan my truth. Most of it anyway. The only part I left out was the way I'd kicked that one woman.

First I told him about Randy's disappearance, how I hadn't lied about finding the girl's body in the back of his truck, how bad it had disturbed me, and how I'd called Detective Morrell and those guys because it was the right thing to do, not because

I wanted Randy to take the fall for something we did together. I told him at that point I wasn't involved at all.

Clutching the backpack on his lap, Ryan gave me a single nod, and I went on.

I asked if he remembered the day the bird bandit dive-bombed me at work. How could he forget that? He and the guys at work talked about it regularly. I told him about the note the bird took, what it said, that I assumed it was a prank set up by him and some of the guys to fuck with me.

He sat perfectly still and listened as I paced in the tiny space in front of the toilet and tub and spewed out a jumbled mess of information about my meetings with Luther and the birds following me and the ruse of investing in EnviroTek. I could tell by the look in his eyes that he had a million questions he wanted to ask, but I didn't give him the chance. I'd finally popped the blister that had been swelling inside my chest for almost two years and I wanted to squeeze out all the pus before I dealt with questions.

I told him everything about Luther. His threats on my family. His ability to manipulate emotions and talk to birds and God knows what else. About the naked man in Colorado. All the jobs I'd done. How the blue jays followed me everywhere, all the time, and could seemingly understand me and pass messages to Luther. Which is why I wanted the blinds closed and TV loud and water on. They were outside waiting. Watching. Listening.

Talking openly about Luther, revealing the truth, made me feel like a huge burden, a huge weight, had been lifted off my chest. The only problem, a fucking huge one that will haunt me until the day I die, was that my burden felt lighter only because some of the weight had been passed to Ryan.

Like any guilt-ridden person trying to rationalize their actions, I explained how I'd tried to use the money to help everyone I could. Him. Brianne. Their mom. My dad. Sera. A pitiful and pathetic excuse, I admitted, but I couldn't do anything else. I had no choice. I had to make the best of the situation and protect my family, right? Wouldn't he do the same? I explained how, although I was uncertain as to how many of the Boulevard girls I'd actually helped dispose of, I'd kept all the flyers and memorized their names, birthdates, and good characteristics out of pure guilt.

Then I told him that when I learned Brianne was pregnant and that Detective Morrell and the cops were suspicious of me, I knew I had to sever ties with Luther somehow. My guilt and fear and paranoia had risen to an unbearable level and knowing I had a new baby coming was the tipping point.

I paused to splash cold water on my face again before telling him his role in all this. I told him that Luther knew he was suspicious of me and had confronted me a few times. That Luther said he was going to kill Ryan after our fight yesterday, but that I'd told him I'd do it myself so he wouldn't have to die the way that man in Colorado did— scared shitless and basically eaten and drank and pecked dry.

After I told him I was supposed to take him out to Plemons and kill him, and that Luther was waiting for us there, he stood up and said, "I need another cigarette."

When he came back into the bathroom, he closed the door, lit up, and flicked on the ventilation fan.

"Do you believe me?" I asked.

"I know you couldn't make up anything like that," he replied. "You don't have a creative bone in your body, and that's one crazy fucking story. So yeah," he locked eyes with me, "I believe you."

"Even the Luther and bird stuff?"

"I know you believe it." A drag. "And if I don't and you're right, then I'm fucked, right?"

I nodded.

"Then of course I believe it." A smirk teased the corners of his mouth but quickly vanished. "I don't like being fucked." A drag. Another brief smirk. Dark humor had always been his answer to stress. "So what are we supposed to do now?"

"You sure you want in on this?" I asked. "We could kill all the birds around here, and you could try to run if you want. Maybe you could take Brianne and Sera and—"

"What kind of life would that be?" he cut in. "A life running scared? Never feeling safe? Everything I know and care about is here in Mercy. I'm not running. It's not an option." He lifted the toilet lid and dropped his cigarette butt in the water. "Besides, I would never do that to you." We held eye contact for a moment, and a hundred unspoken fears and apologies passed between us. Apologies for the fights, doubts, accusations, lies. Fears of the future, the unknown.

He lit another cigarette. Staring at the tattered linoleum floor, he puffed away for a minute or two before I broke the silence. "I'm sorry I got you involved in this. You don't deserve it."

"You don't either." He looked up at me. "But like Forrest Gump said, shit happens sometimes, right?"

I chuckled. He'd mimicked Tom Hank's voice perfectly. "It does," I agreed.

He took a hard drag. "What do you think we should do?"

I grabbed the cigarette, took a puff, passed it back. "We have to try to kill Luther. He's going to kill both of us if we don't."

"*Try* to kill him?"

"Yeah. *Try*. I assume he can die. I mean, nothing on Earth lives forever, right? But I honestly have no idea. Maybe he can't. Maybe he's not from Earth. Or maybe he can heal himself. Maybe he…I don't know…I don't know…but we have to try."

Twenty-Five

Two Fools, One Errand

We stopped at Toot N' Totum on 45th and bought a six-pack and a few burritos before heading out to Plemons. Paranoid of the large cluster of following blue jays, we drove with the windows up and the radio at a decent volume so we could talk freely. Odd thing was, other than Ryan's few comments about the pursuing birds, we didn't talk about Luther or the crude plan we'd hashed out in the bathroom after I'd showed him what was inside the backpack.

Instead, we talked about the gut buster burritos we were eating. Guessed at how many we'd eaten over the years. Speculated for the thousandth time about their contents. Laughed until our eyes watered about the time Ryan tried to eat one for each beer he drank; he puked half of the thirteen all over Dora Dean's chest outside Wizzards that night and dumped the rest in the floorboard of the Chevy ten minutes later. I spent the next month trying to get the smell out of the cab.

I don't know if we didn't discuss Luther because of fear, stupidity, nervousness, confidence, or all of those. But I was glad we didn't. For the thirty minutes it took to reach Plemons Bridge, we talked about dumb stuff that didn't matter. Just like old times. We hadn't had a conversation like that since I'd met Luther. It was relaxing for me, calming, and based on the look in Ryan's eyes, I think it was relaxing for him as well.

After we crossed the bridge, which was lined with blue jays, I drove toward the same spot I'd buried the body the night Ryan had followed me after our argument in the alley and pulled to a stop in a small clearing next to an abandoned water tank, twenty yards from the dry riverbed. Before I killed the engine, I reminded Ryan that he couldn't talk about the birds that were dotting the surrounding mesquite like blue fruit. He was there to get shot in the head and didn't know about the birds or Luther. He winked at me, opened a beer, and got out of the truck. I grabbed the other five beers and followed him to the back of the truck where he lowered the tailgate and we sat down.

I scanned the overcast sky, wishing the clouds would go away. I knew the sun couldn't kill Luther, but I hoped it could weaken him At least a little. We needed any edge we could get. As we drank, I continually scanned the trees, looking for Luther. I knew he was already there. Watching. Listening. Just like the birds. Waiting to see me take another step toward becoming a monster like him. I figured it would delight him to no end to see me kill Ryan. After I'd done it, he'd probably glide over to me and say something like, "I know it's hard the first time, but it's for the best." He would sound genuine and try to look sympathetic, but his ice blue eyes would sparkle with pride and giddiness, betraying his true emotions.

Ryan tossed his empty bottle into the trees, opened another, and gestured at the riverbed. "Remember when it used to have enough water in it to fish?"

I nodded and opened another beer. A dam built in the late nineties had shrunk the river from a steady four-foot depth down to two, and the drought that has ravaged the panhandle for the last five years took those two. Now the cracked soil absorbed every inch of rain without showing anything for it.

"Robert," Ryan said, "one of my mom's boyfriends when was I eight or nine, used to bring me out here on Sunday mornings to fish. I'd never fished before then." He took a long swig. "I remember the first fish I caught was a small catfish. Robert showed me how to gut it, and we ate it right there on the river's edge. I'd never tasted a fish so good." Another swig. "I wonder what ever happened to Robert? He was one of mom's only boyfriends who didn't totally suck balls."

I knew all about Robert. Ryan had told me the fishing story twenty times over the years. Robert had been one of Brianne's favorites, too. She said he was nice and comforting without being fake or gross like some of the other guys. She said that's probably why he didn't last long. Three or four months, tops.

"My dad brought me out here once, too," I said, and chuckled. "Only because my mom forced him to, though. I don't think he said more than five words the entire time we were here." I'd told Ryan this story before, too, but continued. "So I just sat there and thought about Lurth. Imagined I was at a magical river filled with magical beasts. Beasts that would only befriend children. Beasts that would jump out of the water and swallow my dad whole if I wanted them to."

"I was wrong earlier," Ryan said, elbowing my arm. "I forgot about Lurth and all that shit. You do have a creative bone or two in your body."

Half-heartedly moaning, I rubbed my arm, and Ryan realized he'd elbowed my stab wound. "Sorry, man," he said. "I forgot."

I raised my beer and said, "Nothing this can't remedy."

He raised his bottle, and we drank.

"I don't think I'm creative at all," I said. "My mom, now she was creative. I just followed her lead."

Following a long silence, we both finished our second beer and opened a third. As we sat and talked about how shitty the Mercy Sox team was and about Brianne and the baby, I kept scanning the trees, nervous, looking for Luther.

After Ryan finished his third beer and tossed it into the trees, scattering a few of the blue jays, he eyed mine, which was half full. He made a gesture for me to take it down so we could get the plan rolling.

I jiggled my bottle, sloshing the liquid around, feeling as though cement had been injected into my veins. It was go time. I chugged the rest of my beer. When I stood and threw the bottle toward the riverbed, Ryan stretched his arms to the sky and loudly announced that he had to go take a piss. I nodded and made my way to the truck cab to get the gun. Ryan had his hunting knife in his waistband, hidden beneath his White Zombie T-shirt. He had a clove of garlic in his pocket, as did I, and he had a single shot snub-nosed pistol he'd stolen from his mom years earlier in his sock, hidden by his baggy jeans.

The plan to lure Luther out was simple. I was to walk to the edge of the clearing and call him over to look at something. A piece of scrap metal, an animal, whatever. When he bent to look, I was to step behind him and aim the 9MM at the back of his head. But before I fired, he was going to spin around, see the gun, freak out, and attack me. Let me have it. Punch me in the face or gut hard enough to make it look real. Then I would fall on my back, and he would jump on top of me. As we fought and he took the gun from me, I would call out for Luther's help. But that's where our plan ended. When Luther appeared, all bets were off.

The plan took only a minute or two to execute and went exactly as scripted. When Ryan hit me in the face the first time, knocking my lucky Rangers cap off, I dropped to a knee, and when he kicked me in the side, I fell onto my back and he jumped on top of me. As we struggled for control of the 9MM, I called out, "Luther! Luther!" Many of the blue jays were circling above the treetops; some had landed on the ground around us.

Ryan paused, glanced left, right. "What? Who's—"

I slugged him in the gut and called out for Luther again. It was then that I saw Luther in my peripheral vision behind Ryan, approaching fast, crouched low like a stalking cougar. I looked at Ryan and widened my eyes and he knew. Without hesitation, he jerked the 9MM from my hands, turned and fired.

Luther's shoulder jerked back when the bullet struck. He let loose a fierce growl, causing the blue jays to go into a fluttering frenzy much like they had that night in Colorado. Ryan fired again but must have missed because Luther's aggressive pursuit didn't slow. He lunged at Ryan, knocked him off me, and they barrel-rolled into a patch of prairie grass. Another shot went off as I jumped to my feet and rushed toward the backpack that we'd left on the ground beside the driver's door. As Ryan hollered in either pain or adrenaline, I couldn't tell which, I pulled two of the eight-inch wooden stakes out of the backpack and rushed toward Luther.

Luther turned his head sideways as I approached and shifted left when I stabbed. The stake punctured his upper right back rather than the heart-shot I was hoping for. His eyes locked on mine, ablaze with fury, and he growled a terrifying growl. He knew I was involved now. Ryan hadn't bested me. I'd been a willing participant to lure him out. I raised the stake in my left hand, and the blue jays immediately began dive-bombing me, driving their beaks into my flesh. I swatted at the birds with the stake and my free hand as I tried to keep my eyes on Luther.

Abandoning Ryan, who had gone silent, Luther stood, gripping the 9MM in his hand. The shoulder of his Guayabera was ripped and soaked with blood where he'd been shot. A grimace spread across his face as he reached over his shoulder and removed the stake from his back. He was hurting, in pain, injured. Which meant he could probably die. But he was also furious. He'd been betrayed, setup, lied to. By his friend.

In a blur of motion, he spanned the ten yards between us in a blink. He drove his shoulder into my chest and tackled me to the ground. I heard my ribs crack under his weight and my lungs seized up. I opened my mouth in pain and desperation, eager to inhale, needing to scream, but nothing came out.

Luther knocked the stake out of my hand, then slapped me across the face with the 9MM. "You stupid idiot," he said, followed by a second smack. The barrel sliced my skin, peeling back a wide flap of floppy skin. Warm blood dripped onto my neck. A glint shined in Luther's eyes when he spotted the blood. His nostrils flared, and he inhaled loudly. "I'm going to enjoy this," he said. "I'm going to take it nice and slow. And you know what that means for you, friend." The word "friend" fell from his mouth hard and heavy, like a wrecking ball cut loose from twenty feet in the air.

I struggled to shove him off me but couldn't. I don't know how to explain it other than to say his weight seemed more than physical. Maybe I was weakened by fear or dazed by the blows to the head, I don't know, but I couldn't budge him. He wrapped his slender fingers around my wrists and pinned them to the ground. Then he moved his knees up onto my shoulders and held eye contact with me as he forced all the misery he could into me.

A dreadful, relentless sense of doom assaulted my mind,

dominated my thoughts. A deep, unknown sorrow squashed my chest with the strength of a hundred hands, like the day my mom died, the day Esperanza died. An overwhelming sense of irrational fear, nightmarish fear, unreal fear, washed over me, terrorizing my heart the way it had when I was a child and was certain I'd seen a witch poke her head out of my closet. I couldn't breathe. I squeezed my eyes shut and fought down the beer-bile creeping up my throat. Time slowed to a crawl. I was paralyzed, suspended in a state of despair. I wanted to die. I truly wanted to die right then and there.

When I opened my eyes, Luther licked the blood off my cheek and laughed a maniacal laugh. After flashing me his unbreakable smile, he bit into my arm. The blue jays began hopping around my head as his teeth sank in, chirping and eagerly pecking at my neck and arms and legs to get their share of the feast. He ripped out a small chunk of my flesh, spat it out, and drank from the wound on my arm. As he swallowed, the misery and sorrow and fear he was injecting into me grew in intensity.

Physically, I was being eaten alive. Emotionally, I was in absolute agony. Mentally, all hope was lost. I closed my eyes again and tried to imagine Sera and Brianne sitting on the back porch swing with the new baby. I wanted this to be my last thought before I died. At first the image was blurred by the pain and despair, but it eventually solidified, and I saw my girl's bright eyes and smiling faces, the baby's fat cheeks and bald head.

I was focusing on the mental image, ready to die, waiting for Luther to take a chunk out of my neck like he had the naked Colorado man, when I heard another gunshot. I opened my eyes, and Ryan was staggering toward us, favoring his hurt ankle, his snub-nosed pistol outstretched. He was bleeding from the left side of his abdomen from what I assumed was a gunshot wound. Blood drizzled down his nose from a gash on his forehead. Luther craned his neck and bared his teeth at Ryan.

Ryan tossed the pistol aside, pulled out his hunting knife, and like Rocky Balboa encouraging Apollo Creed before the final round of their first fight, gestured for Luther to bring it. Luther dashed from me to Ryan and tackled him so fast I didn't see it actually happen. I only know it happened because Luther was on top of Ryan. When I got to my feet, Ryan jammed his knife into Luther's thigh, and Luther threw his head back and viciously howled. The birds began attacking Ryan's face in response.

Panicked, I searched the ground, looking for the 9MM. I saw it about ten feet away, and as I ran for it, Ryan let out a blood curdling scream. I looked back and saw Luther pull the knife out of Ryan's gut and then run it across Ryan's neck. When I picked up the 9MM and aimed it at Luther's back, I heard an engine approaching behind me. Reflexively, I spun around and pointed the gun at the oncoming truck.

It was a large tan Dodge with a welding rig in the back. The driver had the rugged look of a lifetime manual laborer, a man with oil in his blood. The stick figure in the passenger seat was probably his grunt worker, a newbie barely old enough to grow chin stubble. The rugged driver put the truck in park but stayed inside the cab, staring at me. They were both staring at me.

I glanced over my shoulder and Luther was gone. The blue jays were gone. Ryan's bloody, lifeless body lie in front of the Chevy. His legs were splayed. Both his hands were on his throat. I glanced at the Dodge, at Ryan, back at the truck. They thought I'd killed Ryan. Of course they did. I was pointing a gun at them. I was bloody. I had tears in my eyes. There was a dead body on the ground ten feet away.

Keeping the gun outstretched, I scanned the area for any sign of Luther. All I saw was two blue dots in a mesquite close to the river bed. As I slid my eyes back to the Dodge's driver, I hollered, "What do you want?"

"Why don't you put the gun down?"

"What the fuck do you want?" I hollered in misguided anger. I could feel my face reddening, tears gathering in my eyes.

"We...we...were over at a nearby derrick and heard gunshots and screaming," the driver said. "We just..." he trailed off as I began marching toward him.

"Turn it off," I yelled. He didn't move, but he didn't obey me, either. The newbie ducked down into the floorboard. I fired a shot into the back right tire, and the air hissed out. "Turn it off," I insisted.

The driver complied and then raised his hands in the air. "We didn't mean...we just thought someone needed help. Please, don't shoot us."

"Get out," I said. Tears began falling down my cheeks. When only the driver's door opened, I added, "Both of you. Out. Now."

I took their cell phones and shoes, ordered them to walk out into the middle of the riverbed, and told them to turn around, close their eyes, and count to a thousand.

Repeatedly glancing at the counting workers, I shuffled over to Ryan and knelt beside him. His eyes were open, but unlike the girl I'd found in Randy's truck, he didn't look horrified. He looked like he was still fighting death, had fought it to the end. "I'm sorry," I whispered, laying my hand on his chest. I didn't want to leave him alone. I wanted to stay there with him. But I couldn't. "I'm sorry," I whispered again, taking his hand and squeezing it one solid time. "I'm so sorry. But I have to go."

I picked up my lucky Rangers cap, put it on, and sprinted to the Chevy. Before I got inside and peeled off, I shot out the remaining three tires on the Dodge and threw the worker's cell phones and shoes into the thick mesquite. I felt bad for scaring the shit out of them. I'm sure they're decent guys, but they thought I'd killed Ryan, which made perfect sense based on my actions and the scene. I had no doubt they would've called 911 the second I left. They would've given the cops my description and license plate number, and they might have followed me a ways and told the cops the direction I was headed. I couldn't allow that. Luther would want to punish me for my betrayal, and since he couldn't take his anger out on me at the moment, I knew he'd take it out on the next best thing. A better thing in his eyes probably. My family. Brianne. Sera. Dad. The baby. I had to get home. I couldn't allow Luther to get to Brianne and Sera before I did.

Twenty-Six

Death of the Chevy

As I sped away from Ryan's body, recklessly veering off the dirt road and smacking into mesquites, I pounded the Chevy's warped wheel and cried and yelled obscenities, sorry I'd involved Ryan, that I had taken him with me, that I'd left him there alone, that he'd never get to meet his nephew, never get to hug Brianne again or say "Collier kids always stick together" in unison with her with a goofy smile on his face. I felt horrible, stupid, selfish, ashamed. If I would've gone after Luther alone and he'd killed me, maybe he would've left Ryan alone, moved on and found another patsy. But maybe he would've...I don't know.

I tried calling Brianne's cell phone the second I was on the highway and had a good signal. When she didn't answer, I left her a message, told her to leave the house if she was home, take Sera and go to her mother's apartment. Lock all the doors and wait for me.

Next I tried Sera's cell, and when I got no answer from her either, my heart dropped into my stomach. I feared Luther had already gotten to them. My imagination ran wild with horrible possibilities I didn't want to consider, causing me to push the pedal to the floorboard.

Two miles north of Mercy, going a hundred miles per hour, I was swerving around a Civic, honking like a road-raged lunatic, when smoke began billowing out from under the hood. The heat gauge was topped out. The Chevy groaned and moaned and slowed, forcing me to stop on the shoulder. I screamed, "No," jumped out, and ran to look under the hood.

The smoke was coming from the radiator, which had been on the verge of rusting out on the bottom for years. It must've cracked when I hit one of the mesquites or hard bumps as I sped away from Ryan. It was bone-dry empty. Frantic, I grabbed the 9MM out of the cab and took off running down the shoulder of the road. I didn't close the hood or take the keys out of the ignition or shut the driver's door. I just ran.

When I reached the Toot 'N Totum north of Jefferson, I was slimy with sweat and out of breath. The wounds on my face and arms and neck stung. Each time I inhaled, a sharp pain knifed into my chest where Luther's shoulder had driven into my ribs.

Two cars were outside the store, a Jeep Cherokee and a Camry. I assumed the Camry belonged to the clerk because it was parked on the side of the building and had a full windshield visor propped on the dash to block the sun. After checking all four Camry doors and finding them locked, I used the butt of the gun to punch out the driver's side window, quickly hotwired it (knowledge I learned from one Ryan Collier), and took off.

I drove down the alley behind the store to avoid being seen by anyone inside, and once I was a block away, I turned onto Washington and sped for home, terrified I was too late.

Twenty-Seven

Luther's Truth Versus My Truth

Brianne's Fit was parked in the driveway. A number of blue jays were in the trees and along the gutter on the edge of the roof. I parked curbside in front of the house and sprinted inside, my chest aching with each arm-pump, the 9MM gripped tight in my hand.

The front door was open, the screen door unlocked. I stopped in the foyer and listened to the silence for a moment before calling out Brianne's name. When there was no answer, I walked halfway up the stairs and hollered her name again, then Sera's. No answer. I thought about checking their bedrooms, but the thought that I might find either of them lying in a pool of blood with a horrified death expression frozen on their face kept my legs from moving any farther up the stairs. I wasn't ready for that yet. Maybe they were out back, on the swing.

I run back downstairs, and when I turned into the kitchen stopped dead in my tracks. Brianne and Luther were seated next to one another at the dining table, two glasses of water in front of them. Brianne eyed me with a mixture of all things negative: disgust, anger, fear, disbelief. Luther eyed me with pure, unrestricted delight.

Luther was in black slacks and a white button-up. There was a slight crimson smudge on the shoulder of the shirt where he'd been shot. Comb tracks lined his slicked back hair. A small red spot colored his skin below his right eye. He had his left hand on top of Brianne's right one.

Barefoot and her hair a frizzy mess, Brianne looked as if

she'd just woken up. She was wearing sweatpants and a long Snoopy T-shirt. Her thin lips were pressed together, tight.

I looked out the kitchen window above the sink. "Where's Sera?" My eyes slid back to the table, to Brianne. "Is she here?"

She slightly shook her head.

"Don't worry," Luther said, his tone disturbingly calm, that wide unbreakable grin spread across his face. "She went to a friend's house after school to study for a math test."

I glanced at his hand atop Brianne's, and my grip tightened on the gun handle. "Get your hand off her. This is between you and me."

"I don't think she sees it that way," Luther said.

I made eye contact with Brianne. Her eyes fell to the gun in my hand, ran across the blood and bite wounds and peck marks on my arm, the gash and swelling below my eye on my face. "Whatever he's told you, don't believe him," I said. "He has powers. He's manipulating you." I glared at Luther. "Get your hand off her!"

"She knows everything, Seth. She knows what you did to Randy and the girls...and Ryan...and your dad."

"What are you—" *Dad.* I pointed the gun at him. "What did you do to my dad?!"

"I didn't do anything, Seth. Now relax and put the gun down."

"What did you do to him?!"

"Seth, you know I'm not the one who killed him. Now lower the gun. We don't want anyone else to get hurt." I looked at Brianne. She was terrified, coiled in on herself and pushing against the back of her chair. "Seth, you're scaring your wife. Put the gun down so we can talk." I lowered the gun.

A thick silence fell over the room. Luther kept smiling at me, Brianne staring, scared. I felt like I was made of sand and would collapse with the slightest breath of air. I spread my weak legs farther apart to balance better, gave Brianne my full attention. "I didn't do anything to anyone, Bri. I promise. I didn't kill anyone." I pointed the 9MM at Luther. "He did. He's the monster. Look what he did to my arm." I held it out. "He tried to fucking eat me."

Brianne shook her head in disbelief. "You're delusional, Seth. You need help. You don't know what you're saying. He's a detective. His name is Jayson. He's not a monster." She placed her left hand over her belly, and her eyes welled up. "How could you do it?" she asked. "How could you kill Ryan? He loved you. Looked up to you. All he ever wanted was your approval."

"I didn't kill him. And…and…" My mind stuttered, glitched, which made me appear even more guilty and crazy. It was just too hard to straighten out all of Luther's lies in my head much less deliver them verbally in a coherent manner. I pointed the 9MM at Luther again. "He killed Ryan. Not me. And…and…I tried to stop him." I shook my head. "And he's not a detective. His name is Luther and he's some kind of monster. A vampire or alien…or something. By touching your hand he's making you feel—" I broke off when Luther leaned over and whispered something in Brianne's ear.

"What did you tell her?" I stepped forcefully forward. "What did you tell her?!"

"The truth, Seth. The truth."

"Your truth is not my truth, Luther." I wanted to knock that shitty, pompous grin off his face. Shoot it off.

"Just relax, Seth. Calm down. You know my name's not Luther. It's Detective Jayson Jakes. I work with Detective Morrell and Sergeant Adair. You know that. I've spoken to you several times over the past year, remember? We talked about Randy and the missing girls."

"You're a liar," I said through gritted teeth.

Brianne's eyes stayed locked on me as tears ran down her pregnancy-rounded cheeks.

"Don't get angry. I'm here to help you," Luther said. "Somewhere deep down you know Luther doesn't exist. You know he's a just figment of your imagination. An alter ego. Someone your subconscious invented so you could deal with your actions. It's okay to admit it. Sometimes people's minds collapse. Like what happened to your dad. It's not your fault."

"Bullshit! You are Luther. You forced me to bury those girls."

"It's time to stop the lies and self-deception. You know that you and Randy kidnapped and killed those girls. You got rid of Randy and tried to blame him for everything. You killed Ryan because he was getting too close to figuring out the truth. And you killed your dad because he found Randy's wallet and pocketknife in his garage and questioned you about it. Just admit it, Seth. We have a strong case against you. We know you've been burying the bodies on your construction sites. You're going to jail. The least you could do is tell Brianne the truth because she..." he lay his hand on her belly, his slender thumb gently moving back and forth. "And this baby deserves that much."

"The truth? *The truth?*" I met eyes with Brianne and saw not a woman but a terrified little girl. Someone whose mind and emotions were teetering on the edge of a cliff. "Brianne, I didn't do it. He's lying. I swear. He's a fucking monster. *The* Boulevard Monster. He made me—"

She slowly shook her head. "Don't," she whispered. "Don't. Ryan was right when he thought you were hiding something. I was right when I questioned your actions before the wedding. The signs were all there. Don't lie. Not anymore. Please. The only monster here is you, Seth. You. You need help."

"Brianne." I begged her with my eyes, lowered my tone to a personal, sensitive level only she knew. "You know me. You *know* me." I tapped my chest, although looking back, I shouldn't have done it with the gun. "You know I would never hurt anyone. He made me bury the bodies. He told me that if I didn't he'd kill you and Ryan and anyone else I loved. I had no choice." Tears began falling down my cheeks. I felt like a giant wall inside my chest holding my emotions at bay had collapsed. "But when you told me you were pregnant, I knew I had to break ties with him. I decided I was going to try and kill him. It was the only way. But then Ryan confronted me and..." I trialed off when Brianne closed her eyes, her head drooped, and she covered her ears with her hands. She didn't believe me. There was nothing I could say to change that. She'd heard enough, hurt enough. "Bri...Bri?"

She wept, loud. I'd never seen her cry that hard. It stung to hear it. Luther stroked the back of her head, ran his fingers through her hair—what I should have been doing. He loved watching me hurt watching her hurt. I should've known he wouldn't have just killed her before I arrived. That wouldn't have been painful enough. "It'll be all right," he said. "I know the truth hurts." He cut his eyes at me. "But it's all over now. He won't be able to hurt you anymore."

He winked at me—fucking winked at me—and a rage exploded inside my chest. I aimed far enough left that Brianne wouldn't be in danger and fired at him. She screamed and toppled back in her chair, hitting her head against the wall. She crashed onto her belly and her sobs ceased.

Luther nudged her with his foot. She was out cold. "Now it's just you and me," he said, his blue eyes aglow with devilish desire. "But don't worry, I'll deal with her later."

With a guttural, animalistic howl, I quickly covered the short distance between us, firing the 9MM again and again and again. I hit him once in the thigh, and once in the same shoulder he'd already been shot in, and although he jerked back with each hit, he didn't go down. In fact, his eyes never left mine. I dropped the gun and lunged at him as he bared his teeth. We crashed into the dining table, flipping it over on top of us. The glasses shattered on the floor. My lucky Rangers hat flew off.

I scrambled on top of him and jammed my thumb into one of the bullet wounds in his shoulder. As I was reaching my other hand for his neck, I could hear blue jays chirping outside, some slamming into the double-paned kitchen window. Luther wrapped his hand around my wrist and took control of me.

For the second time that afternoon, I was paralyzed by the power of emotions that I didn't want, didn't need, couldn't control, couldn't handle. Luther pulled my thumb out of his bullet wound, and my eyes rolled back in my head as my heart and thoughts were consumed by any and everything dreadful—hurt, terror, paranoia, doom, depression. All at once.

My arms and legs trembled, and Luther let go of my wrist and shoved me off of him. I rolled onto my back, two or three feet away from Brianne. As the horrible feelings slowly receded and I regained control of my thoughts and emotional core, I glanced over at Brianne. Her eyes were closed, but I could tell she was breathing. The hairs dangling over her nose flared with each exhale.

I moved the hairs away from her nose and touched her cheek. "I'm sorry, Bri," I whispered. "I'm so sorry."

When Luther cackled, I snapped my head and saw him standing over me, staring down at me. The birds were still slamming into the kitchen window, and it was cracking.

Luther slowly knelt on top of me. "You had it so good, Seth. I gave you the opportunity of a lifetime, and you blew it."

"You ruined me," I said. "You forced me to turn into a monster."

"I forced you to become a man who could take care of his family. Better his family." He tapped his own chest. "I gave you the opportunity the world wouldn't. And what did you give me in return?"

"I can't live the way you want me to live."

"You betrayed me." He lowered his face to within an inch of mine. His breath smelled of copper and lavender, blood and spring. "I thought you would be different. I thought you understood. I thought we could be friends."

"I understand as well as any sane human ever will. You're a monster, and part of me does feel sorry for you. But a larger part of me hates everything you stand for. You don't have to live the way you live. Kill the way you kill. You could use your abilities for so much more."

Enraged, Luther leaned over and took a chunk of flesh out of my shoulder. I put my hands on either side of his head but couldn't pry him loose. When he rose up, he met eyes with me and spit the chunk at my face. "I'm going to make this nice and long. Even after you die, you'll hurt from my wrath."

He moved forward as if he were about to kiss me, but instead sunk his teeth into my left cheek, a few inches from the corner of my mouth. I howled in pain and began pummeling him in the ribs with my fists, but it didn't seem to faze him. He spat a small chunk of my cheek at Brianne this time, then bit down on my collar bone and began sucking.

I turned my head toward Brianne. I didn't care if I died, but I couldn't leave her here with him. Leave our baby vulnerable to Luther's sordid desires. God knows what he'd do to a soft, supple, fresh....no...no...I can't go there. Holy shit, I can't go there.

I gathered all the strength I could, reared back, and punched him in the head. He rose up and sneered at me with my warm blood on his lips and teeth. In the distance, I could hear bird's slamming into other windows in the house. Possibly the front and back doors, too. Luther backhanded me hard enough to momentarily knock me out.

When I came to, he was sucking on my collar bone again. I turned my head and looked at Brianne. Wanting to feel her skin one more time before I died, I slid my hand across the floor toward her face and felt a large shard of glass, a piece of one of the glasses that had been on the table. I squeezed my hand around the shard hard enough to cut my palm, then in an arcing motion, rammed it into Luther's neck.

Surprised, he shot upright and brought his hand up to the glass as I rammed it deeper into his neck with the palm of my hand. He toppled off of me, wide-eyed and grasping for the shard. The kitchen window finally shattered and birds swarmed in as I scrabbled backwards toward the kitchen sink. I quickly retrieved a knife from a drawer, ran at Luther, and stabbed him in the chest over and over and over. I stabbed him twenty good times as blue jays attacked me, pecking at my arms and head and back.

The glow in Luther's eyes faded as his pupils dilated, eclipsing the piercing blue iris. Continually swatting at the attacking birds, I watched him until his chest stopped heaving. Then—I know this will sound grotesque, but I promised myself I'd tell everything, tell the truth—I grabbed his hair to hold his head steady and sawed off his head. I had to make sure he was dead, had to assure he couldn't hurt Brianne or Sera or the baby ever again.

When I finished, I rolled Brianne onto her back to make sure she was still breathing and there was no blood or moisture between her legs. As I checked her, some of the bird's latched onto Luther's hair and lifted his head into the air. I jumped up and grabbed it before they reached the kitchen window, pried it away from them, ran to the garage, slammed and locked the door.

I dropped the head on the cement floor, and as I doused it with gasoline and set it on fire, birds started slamming into the windows lining the top of the garage door and the birds inside the house started slamming into the locked door leading into the garage. I watched Luther's hair disappear and his skin melt and his eyes swell and blacken. When the smoke was too thick for me to breathe easily or see clearly, I opened the garage door. Five or six blue jays swooped in and grabbed what remained of the smoldering head with their talons and flew back out, some of their feathers catching fire as they went.

I made my way back into the kitchen just in time to see Luther's body being dragged out of the kitchen window by twenty or thirty blue jays. They had him by the pants and shirt and skin—whatever they could get their beaks or talons on. After they had him out in an open area in the backyard, they lifted him off the ground high enough to clear the fence and trees and then flew away, headed toward the open plains behind the house.

I had no idea where they were taking him, and I didn't care. I only cared about Brianne. I lifted her off the ground and carried her to the stolen Camry. She was moaning when I belted her into the passenger seat. I rubbed her cheeks and tried to talk to her for a moment, but she only moaned. I held my hand on her belly, begging God for a sign. Finally, thankfully, after a lifetime of anxiety had looped through my body and was starting a second lap, I felt the baby jerk or kick or something. He was alive.

I kissed Brianne's forehead, and then ran inside and grabbed the 9MM and my lucky Rangers hat. On my way back to the car, I also grabbed Brianne's laptop off the coffee table.

I noticed a couple of blue jays trailing us on the way to Mercy General despite the light rain that had started falling from the overcast sky. I talked to Brianne as I drove, trying to get her to respond, to open her eyes, to tell me she was okay. She occasionally moaned, but she never moved or regained consciousness.

I parked in the drop-off/pick-up area, scooped Brianne out of the car and hurried inside. The second the sliding glass doors parted, a nurse sprinted toward us with a wheel chair. She paused a few feet in front of us and looked me up and down, obviously taken back by my appearance. I looked like I'd just stepped out of a zombie movie. I was slick with sweat, had swollen lips and eyes, chunks of flesh missing from my cheeks and arm, peck marks that looked like bloody chicken pocks all over my arms and neck, and blood—Luther's and my own—all over my clothes and body. And I was carrying an unconscious woman who was eight months pregnant.

I placed Brianne in the wheelchair and took a step back.

"What happened to her?" the nurse asked.

"She fell and hit her head," I replied. My voice sounded weak, untrustworthy, pathetic and guilty. I could feel all the eyes in the waiting room on me, scrutinizing me. One lady in a nearby chair held up her cell phone and snapped a picture. "I haven't been able to wake her," I said. "But she's breathing and moaning. And I felt the baby moving, too."

"What's her name?" the nurse asked, eying me with a healthy dose of skepticism. She'd probably heard the *she-fell-and-hit-her-head* a hundred times, and more often than not, it probably turned out a lie.

"Her name's Brianne."

"How many months along is she?"

"Eight. Eight months."

The nurse looked me up and down again, and it seemed like she wanted to ask me if I was all right, what had happened to me, but she didn't. She stepped behind the wheelchair and pushed Brianne toward a long hallway behind her. After taking a few steps, she looked back over her shoulder at me. "You need to go over to that desk in the corner and fill out some paperwork."

I nodded, and then scanned the waiting room. Each time I met eyes with anyone, they looked away. At the end of the hallway the nurse stopped and talked to a man in a white coat. She turned and pointed my direction, and he nodded and headed my way.

I wanted to fill out the paperwork. I wanted to follow Brianne to her room and make sure she and the baby would be okay. I wanted to be there holding her hand when she woke up. I wanted to tell her the truth, what she missed after she was knocked unconscious. I wanted her to believe me. I knew that once I left I'd never see her again. But I couldn't stay. Cops would be there to question me any second. I couldn't risk that. I had to be content knowing that she was in good hands.

I ran out of the hospital, jumped in the Camry, and sped away. In my rearview mirror, I saw a couple of nurses run out into the rain after me, waving their arms in the air, yelling for me to stop, to come back.

I ditched the Camry shortly after I left the hospital. I left it in an elementary school parking lot, broke into and hotwired an old Explorer parked roadside a block away, then left Mercy for the final time.

I drove north and stopped in a small, nondescript town called Sunray, left the Explorer in front of a vacant house in a seemingly abandoned neighborhood behind a Dairy Queen, and then walked to a cheap trucker motel on the edge of town. WI-FI and CABLE the roadside marquee read, minus the F and L.

A big lady in a blue-flower muu-muu sitting behind the motel's front desk was watching a soap opera on a small TV. She never looked me directly in the eye. I'd put on a jacket that I'd found in the Explorer to hide my arms. I kept my hat low and my head down to hide my face wounds as best as I could. She asked for my ID, but when I told her I'd been robbed the day before and didn't have it, she said as long as I was paying cash it didn't matter.

I handed her all the cash I had, enough to secure the room for six days if needed.

Twenty-Eight

Last Call

Every time I've taken a break from typing and peeked out of the blinds at the motel's parking lot, I've seen more and more blue jays hanging around. Watching. Listening.

I don't know if the birds are now working for other Luthers that may be out there, or if they were simply set on a mission by Luther and won't deviate from it without orders—orders they'll never receive. I'm so tired and broken I really don't care anymore. I haven't eaten in four days, and my sleep has come in random, fitful spurts, infected with nightmares.

My only contact with the outside world has come via TV and the Mercy Monitor online. The day I dropped Brianne off at the hospital, they found my dad, dead in his house. There had been no forced entry, and his throat had been slit by a large pocketknife they believe belonged to Randy. I'm the prime suspect. They think Dad stumbled onto information linking me to some of the girl's murders and Randy's disappearance. Citing leaks from inside the Mercy Police Department, Michelle Farmer reported that along with the pocketknife, Randy's wallet was found at the scene. Just like Luther had told Brianne.

I hope Dad wasn't scared when Luther came knocking. I'd like to think he was having one of those days where he believed he was back in Vietnam, smack dab in the middle of a jungle, in the middle of a nasty war. If he was having one of those days, he would've been on high alert and given Luther one hell of a fight. In his heart and mind, he would have died fighting for his country, a great sense of pride for him.

Ryan's body was recovered after the two oil field workers

made their way back to town. Michelle Farmer interviewed both of them on last night's news. The interview was hyped as *The Two Men Who Came Face-to-Face with the Boulevard Monster*. They told her they'd heard me fighting with Ryan, then heard gunshots and screams, and then...you know. A memorial service was held for Ryan and my dad at the same church where Brianne and I were married, and they were both buried at Harrington Cemetery yesterday.

I'm sure the cops have interviewed Brianne, too, but nothing about those talks has come out in the media yet. What did come out, though, thank God, is that my son (they didn't mention a name if Brianne has given him one) was born a day and a half ago. Although four weeks early and smaller than the doctors would've liked, he was healthy and doing well according to the Monitor.

This morning Detective Morrell held another press conference at the police station. He said they'd already recovered two of the missing Boulevard girls from construction sites, and he was certain they'd find the rest soon. During the question segment of the conference, some reporter asked him what he would say to me if he could talk to me. He aimed his droopy, basset hound eyes at the camera, and in his typical monotonous tone said, "Seth, it's all over. Turn yourself in. Please. We don't want anyone else to get hurt."

I have no intention of turning myself in. It would serve no purpose. Like I said earlier, even if I retained the best lawyer Mercy has to offer, I would be found guilty. No matter how detailed my account, no matter how hard I tried to convey my true intentions, my testimony would sound too contrived, too incredible, for sensible ears. Jurors would never believe me. They would see me as a murderous, lying nutcase, and I'd spend my last days leading up to my execution behind bars, with psychologists fighting to dissect me, to figure out the true reason behind my delusions of a monster named Luther and his devilish birds.

On top of that, Brianne and Sera would be forced to sit through a heart-wrenching trial that could drag out for years. They would have to testify and would possibly be accused of knowing more than they do. They don't deserve that. I won't put them through it. I don't know exactly what I'll do when I finish this, but I do know I won't allow myself to be caught.

I have options.

I have a length of rope I found in the back of the Explorer.

I have my 9MM and five more bullets.

Or, if I want, I'm sure the blue jays out in the parking lot would help. They look angry, and hungry.

For My Girls, Brianne and Sera

I admit I've made some bad decisions over the past few years, terrible ones in fact, selfish ones, but I am NOT the Boulevard Monster. I'm a concerned, loving, hard-working husband and father who felt cornered and did everything he had to do in order to protect his family. Nothing more, nothing less.

I know I don't have all the answers you want. Hell, I don't have half the answers I want. But I've given you everything I have. Everything I saw. Everything I heard. Everything I thought. Everything I felt. I hope knowing my side of the story, my truth, will help you deal with the scrutiny and questions coming your way. I hope it will help you have less hatred in your hearts when you think about me.

I don't expect your forgiveness, but please know, please believe, that I'm truly sorry for the pain I've put you through. I never meant to hurt you. I never meant for Ryan, or Dad, or anyone else to die.

I love you both with all my heart.

I hope we'll see each other again on Lurth someday, like we've talked about.

Take care of each other and the baby.

About the Author

Jeremy Hepler is the Bram Stoker-nominated author of THE BOULEVARD MONSTER, CRICKET HUNTERS, SUNRAY ALICE, and numerous short stories and nonfiction articles. He lives in central Texas with his wife and son and is currently working on his next novel. For more information, you can find him on Twitter, Facebook, Instagram, Goodreads, or Amazon.

Curious about other Crossroad Press books?
Stop by our site:
http://store.crossroadpress.com
We offer quality writing
in digital, audio, and print formats.